The Bride of Fort Edward: Founded on an Incident of the Revolution

by Delia Salter Bacon

PERSONS INTRODUCED.

British and American officers and soldiers.

Indians employed in the British service.

ELLISTON—*A religious missionary residing in the adjacent woods.*

GEORGE GREY—*A young American.*

LADY ACKLAND—*Wife of an English Officer.*

MARGARET—*Her maid.*

MRS. GREY—*The widow of a Clergyman residing near Fort Edward.*

HELEN, *and* ANNIE,—*Her daughters.*

JANETTE—*A Canadian servant.*

Children, &c.

Time included—from the afternoon of one day to the close of the following.

PART I. THE CRISIS AND ITS VICTIM

PART II. LOVE

PART III. FATE

PART IV. FULFILMENT

PART V. FULFILMENT

PART VI. RECONCILIATION

THE BRIDE OF FORT EDWARD.

PART FIRST.

INDUCTION.

DIALOGUE I.

SCENE. *The road-side on the slope of a wooded hill near Fort Edward. The speakers, two young soldiers,—Students in arms.*

1st Student. These were the evenings last year, when the bell
From the old college tower, would find us still
Under the shady elms, with sauntering step
And book in hand, or on the dark grass stretched,
Or lounging on the fence, with skyward gaze
Amid the sunset warble. Ah! that world,—
That world we lived in then—where is it now?
Like earth to the departed dead, methinks.

2nd Stud. Yet oftenest, of that homeward path I think,
Amid the deepening twilight slowly trod,
And I can hear the click of that old gate,
As once again, amid the chirping yard,
I see the summer rooms, open and dark,
And on the shady step the sister stands,
Her merry welcome, in a mock reproach,
Of Love's long childhood breathing. Oh this year,
This year of blood hath made me old, and yet,
Spite of my manhood now, with all my heart,
I could lie down upon this grass and weep
For those old blessed times, the times of peace again.

1st Stud. There will be weeping, Frank, from older eyes,
Or e'er again that blessed time shall come.
Hearts strong and glad now, must be broke ere then:
Wild tragedies, that for the days to come

Shall faery pastime make, must yet ere then
Be acted here; ay, with the genuine clasp
Of anguish, and fierce stabs, not buried in silk robes,
But in hot hearts, and sighs from wrung souls' depths.
And they shall walk in light that we have made,
They of the days to come, and sit in shadow
Of our blood-reared vines, not counting the wild cost.
Thus 'tis: among glad ages many,—one—
In garlands lies, bleeding and bound. Times past,
And times to come, on ours, as on an altar—
Have laid down their griefs, and unto us
Is given the burthen of them all.

2nd Stud.   And yet,
See now, how pleasantly the sun shines there
Over the yellow fields, to the brown fence
Its hour of golden beauty—giving still.
And but for that faint ringing from the fort,
That comes just now across the vale to us,
And this small band of soldiers planted here,
I could think this was peace, so calmly there,
The afternoon amid the valley sleeps.

1st Stud. Yet in the bosom of this gentle time,
The crisis of an age-long struggle heaves.

2nd Stud. Age-long?—Why, this land's history can scarce
Be told in ages, yet.

1st Stud.   But this war's can.
In that small isle beyond the sea, Francis,
Ages, ages ago, its light first blazed.
This is the war. Old, foolish, blind prerogative,
In ermines wrapped, and sitting on king's thrones;
Against young reason, in a peasant's robe
His king's brow hiding. For the infant race
Weaves for itself the chains its manhood scorns,
(When time hath made them adamant, alas!—)
The reverence of humanity, that gold
Which makes power's glittering round, ordained of God
But for the lovely majesty of right,
Unto a mad usurper, yielding, all,
Making the low and lawless will of man
Vicegerent of that law and will divine,
Whose image only, reason hath, on earth.
This is the struggle:—*here*, we'll fight it out.
'Twas all too narrow and too courtly *there*;
In sight of that old pageantry of power

We were, in truth, the children of the past,
Scarce knowing our own time: but here, we stand
In nature's palaces, and we are *men*;—
Here, grandeur hath no younger dome than this;
And now, the strength which brought us o'er the deep,
Hath grown to manhood with its nurture here,—
Now that they heap on us abuses, that
Had crimsoned the first William's cheek, to name,—
We're ready now—for our last grapple with blind power.

[*Exeunt.*

DIALOGUE II.

SCENE. *The same. A group of ragged soldiers in conference.*

1st Soldier. I am flesh and blood myself, as well as the rest of you, but there is no use in talking. What the devil would you do?—You may talk till dooms-day, but what's to hinder us from serving our time out?— and that's three months yet. Ay, there's the point. Show me that.

2nd Sol. Three months! Ha, thank Heaven mine is up to-morrow; and, I'll tell you what, boys, before the sun goes down to-morrow night, you will see one Jack Richards trudging home,—trudging home, Sirs! None of your bamboozling, your logic, and your figures. A good piece of bread and butter is the figure for me. But you should hear the Colonel, though, as the time draws nigh. Lord! you'd think I was the General at least. Humph, says I.

3d Sol. Ay, ay,—feed you on sugar-candy till they get you to sign, and then comes the old shoes and moccasins.—

2nd Sol. And that's true enough, Ned. I've eaten myself, no less than two very decent pair in the service. I'll have it out of Congress yet though, I'll be hanged if I don't. None of your figures for me! I say, boys, I am going home.

1st Sol. Well, go home, and—can't any body else breathe? Why don't you answer me, John?—What would you have us do?—

4th Sol. Ask Will Wilson there.

1st Sol. Will?—Where is he?

4th Sol. There he stands, alongside of the picket there, his hands in his pockets, whistling, and looking as wise as the dragon. Mind you, there's always something pinching at the bottom of that same whistle, though its such a don't-care sort of a whistle too. Ask Will, he'll tell you.

3d Sol. Ay, Will has been to the new quarters to-day. See, he's coming this way.

5th Sol. And he saw Striker there, fresh from the Jerseys, come up along with that new General there, yesterday.

3d Sol. General Arnold?

5th Sol. Ay, ay, General Arnold it is.

6th Sol. [*Advancing.*] I say, boys—

4th Sol. What's the matter, Will?

6th Sol. Do you want to know what they say below?

All. Ay, ay, what's the news?

6th Sol. All up there, Sirs. A gone horse!—and he that turns his coat first, is the best fellow.

4th Sol. No?

6th Sol. And shall I tell you what else they say?

4th Sol. Ay.

6th Sol. Shall I?

All. Ay, ay. What is it?

6th Sol. That we are a cowardly, sneaking, good-for-nothing pack of poltroons, here in the north. There's for you! There's what you get for your pains, Sirs. And for the rest, General Schuyler is to be disgraced, and old Gates is to be set over us again, and—no matter for the rest. See here, boys. Any body coming? See here.

3d Sol. What has he got there?

2nd Sol. The Proclamation! The Proclamation! Will you be good enough to let me see if there is not a picture there somewhere, with an Indian and a tomahawk?

6th Sol. Now, Sirs, he that wants a new coat, and a pocket full of money—

3d Sol. That's me fast enough.

2nd Sol. If he had mentioned a shirt-sleeve now, or a rim to an old hat—

4th Sol. Or a bit of a crown, or so.

6th Sol. He that wants a new coat—get off from my toes, you scoundrel.

All. Let's see. Let's see. Read—read.

7th Sol. (*Spouting.*) "And he that don't want his house burned over his head, and his wife and children, or his mother and sisters, as the case may be, butchered or eaten alive before his eyes—"

3d Sol. Heavens and earth! It 'ant so though, Wilson, is it?

7th Sol. "Is required to present himself at the said village of Skeensborough, on or before the 20th day of August next. Boo—boo—boo—Who but I. Given under my hand."—If it is not *it*—it is something very like it, I can tell you, Sirs. I say, boys, the old rogue wants his neck wrung for insulting honest soldiers in that fashion; and I say that you—for shame, Will Willson.

4th Sol. Hush!—the Colonel!—Hush!

2nd Sol. And who is that proud-looking fellow, by his side?

4th Sol. Hush! General Arnold. He's a sharp one—roll it up—roll it up.

6th Sol. Get out,—you are rumpling it to death.

(*Two American officers are seen close at hand, in a bend of the ascending road; the soldiers enter the woods.*)

DIALOGUE III.

SCENE. *The same.*

1st Officer. I cannot conceal it from you, Sir; there is but one feeling about it, as far as I can judge, and I had some chances in my brief journey—

2nd Off. Were you at head-quarters?

1st Off. Yes,—and every step of this retreating army only makes it more desperate. I never knew any thing like the mad, unreasonable terror this army inspires. Burgoyne and his Indians!—"*Burgoyne and the Indians*"—there is not a girl on the banks of the Connecticut that does not expect to see them by her father's door ere day-break. Colonel Leslie, what were those men concealing so carefully as we approached just now?—Did you mark them?

2nd Off. Yes. If I am not mistaken, it was the paper we were speaking of.

1st Off. Ay, ay,—I thought as much.

2nd Off. General Arnold, I am surprised you should do these honest men the injustice to suppose that such an impudent, flimsy, bombastic tirade as that same proclamation of Burgoyne's, should have a feather's weight with any mother's son of them.

Arnold. A feather's, ay a feather's, just so; but when the scales are turning, a feather counts too, and that is the predicament just now of more minds than you think for, Colonel Leslie. A pretty dark horizon around us just now, Sir,—another regiment goes off to-morrow, I hear. Hey?

Leslie. Why, no. At least we hope not. We think we shall be able to keep them yet, unless—that paper might work some mischief with them perhaps, and it would be rather a fatal affair too, I mean in the way of example.—These Green Mountain Boys—

Arnold. Colonel Leslie, Colonel Leslie, this army is melting away like a snow-wreath. There's no denying it. Your General misses it. The news of one brave battle would send the good blood to the fingers' ends from ten thousand chilled hearts; no matter how fearful the odds; the better, the better,—no matter how large the loss;—for every slain soldier, a hundred better would stand on the field;—

Leslie. But then—

Arnold. By all that's holy, Sir, if I were head here, the red blood should smoke on this grass ere to-morrow's sunset. I would have battle here, though none but the birds of the air were left to carry the tale to the nation. I tell you, Colonel Leslie, a war, whose resources are only in the popular feeling, as now, and for months to come, this war's must be; a war, at least, which depends wholly upon the *unselfishness* of a people, as this war does, can be kept alive by excitement only. It was wonderful enough indeed, to behold a whole people, the low and comfort-loving too, in whose narrow lives that little world which the sense builds round us, takes such space, forsaking the tangible good of their merry firesides, for rags and wretchedness,—poverty that the thought of the citizen beggar cannot reach,—the supperless night on the frozen field; with the news perchance of a home in ashes, or a murdered household, and, last of all, on some dismal day, the edge of the sword or the sharp bullet ending all;—and all in defence of—what?— an idea—an abstraction,—a thought:—I say this was wonderful enough, even in the glow of the first excitement. But now that the Jersey winter is fresh in men's memories, and Lexington and Bunker Hill are forgotten, and all have found leisure and learning to count the cost; it were expecting miracles indeed, to believe that this army could hold together with a policy like this. Every step of this retreat, I say again, treads out some lingering spark of enthusiasm. Own it yourself. Is not this army dropping off by hundreds, and desertion too, increasing every hour, thinning your own ranks and swelling your foes?—and that, too, at a crisis—Colonel Leslie, retreat a little further, some fifty miles further; let Burgoyne once set foot in Albany, and the business is done,—we may roll up our pretty declaration as fast as we please, and go home in peace.

Leslie. General Arnold, I have heard you to the end, though you have spoken insultingly of councils in which I have had my share. Will you look at this little clause in this paper, Sir. The excitement you speak of will come ere long, and that at a rate less ruinous than this whole army's loss. There's a line—there's a line, Sir, that will make null and void, very soon, if not on the instant, all the evil of these golden promises. There'll be excitement enough ere long; but better blood than that shed in battle fields must flow to waken it.

Arnold. I hardly understand you, Sir. Is it this threat you point at?

Leslie. Can't you see?—They have let loose these hell-hounds upon us, and butchery must be sent into our soft and innocent homes;—beings that we have sheltered from the air of heaven, brows that have grown pale at the breath of an ungentle word, must meet the red knife of the Indian now. Oh God, this is war!

Arnold. I understand you, Colonel Leslie. There was a crisis like this in New Jersey last winter, I know, when our people were flocking to the royal standard, as they are now, and a few fiendish outrages on the part of the foe changed the whole current in our favor. It may be so now, but meanwhile—

Leslie. Meanwhile, this army is the hope of the nation, and must be preserved. We are wronged, Sir. Have we not done all that men could do? What were twenty pitched battles to such an enemy, with a force like ours, compared with the harm we have done them? Have we not kept them loitering here among these hills, wasting the strength that was meant to tell in the quivering fibres of men, on senseless trees and stones, paralyzing them with famine, wearying them with unexciting, inglorious toil, until, divided and dispirited, at last we can measure our power with theirs, and fight, not in vain? Why, even now the division is planning there, which will bring them to our feet. And what to us, Sir, were the hazards of one bloody encounter, to the pitiful details of this unhonored warfare?—We are wronged—we are wronged, Sir.

Arnold. There is some policy in the plan you speak of,—certainly, there is excellent policy in it if one had the patience to follow it out; but then you can't make Congress see it, or the people either; and so, after all, your General is superseded. Well, well, at all events he must abandon this policy now,—it's the only chance left for him.

Leslie. Why; howso?

Arnold. Or else, don't you see?—just at the point where the glory appears, this eastern hero steps in, and receives it all; and the laurels which he has been rearing so long, blow just in time to drop on the brow of his rival.

Leslie. General Arnold,—excuse me, Sir—you do not understand the man of whom you speak. There is a substance in the glory he aims at, to which, all that you call by the name is as the mere shell and outermost rind. Good Heavens! Do you think that, for the sake of his own individual fame, the man would risk the fate of this great enterprize?—What a mere fool's bauble, what an empty shell of honor, would that be. If I thought he would—

Arnold. It might be well for you to lower your voice a little, Sir; the gentleman of whom you are speaking is just at hand.

[*Other officers are seen emerging from the woods.*]

3d Off. Yes, if this rumor holds, Lieutenant Van Vechten, your post is likely to become one of more honor than safety. Gentlemen—Ha!—General Arnold! You are heartily welcome;—I have been seeking you, Sir. If this news is any thing, the movement that was planned for Wednesday, we must anticipate somewhat.

Leslie. News from the enemy, General?

Gen. Schuyler. Stay—those scouts must be coming in, Van Vechten. Why, we can scarce call it news yet, I suppose; but if this countryman's tale is true, Burgoyne himself, with his main corps, is encamping at this moment at the Mills, scarce three miles above us.

Arnold. Ay, and good news too.

Leslie. But that cannot be, Sir—Alaska—

Gen. Schuyler. Alaska has broken faith with us if it is, and the army have avoided the delay we had planned for them.—That may be.—This man overheard their scouts in the woods just below us here.

Arnold. And if it is,—do you talk of retreat, General Schuyler? In your power now it lies, with one hour's work perchance, to make those lying enemies of yours in Congress eat the dust, to clear for ever your blackened fame. Why, Heaven itself is interfering to do you right, and throwing honor in your way as it were! Do you talk of retreat, Sir, now?

Gen. Schuyler. Heaven has other work on hand just now, than righting the wrongs of such heroes as you and I, Sir. Colonel Arnold—I beg your pardon, Sir, Congress has done you justice at last I see,—General Arnold, you are right as to the consequence, yet, for all that, if this news is true, I must order the retreat. My reputation I'll trust in God's hands. My honor is in my own keeping.

[*Exeunt Schuyler, Leslie, and Van Vechten.*

Arnold. There's a smoke from that chimney; are those houses inhabited, my boy?

Boy. Part of them, Sir. Some of our people went oft to-day. That white house by the orchard—the old parsonage there? Ay, there are ladies there Sir, but I heard Colonel Leslie saying this morning 'twas a sin and a shame for them to stay another hour.

Arnold. Ay, Ay. I fancied the Colonel was not dealing in abstractions just now.

[*Exeunt.*

DIALOGUE IV.

SCENE. *A room in the Parsonage,—an old-fashioned summer parlor.—-On the side a door and windows opening into an orchard, in front, a yard filled with shade trees. The view beyond bounded by a hill partly wooded. A young girl, in the picturesque costume of the time, lies sleeping on the antique sofa. Annie sits by a table, covered with coarse needlework, humming snatches of songs as she works.*

Annie, (singing.)
  Soft peace spreads her wings and flies weeping away.
  Soft peace spreads her wings and flies weeping away.
  And flies weeping away.
    The red cloud of war o'er our forest is scowling,
  Soft peace spreads her wings and flies weeping away.
  Come blow the shrill bugle, the war dogs are howling,
  Already they eagerly snuff out their prey—
    The red cloud of war—the red cloud of war—

Yes, let me see now,—with a little plotting this might make two—two, at least,—and then—

  The red cloud of war o'er our forest is scowling,
  Soft peace spreads her wings and flies weeping away,
    The infants affrighted cling close to their mothers,
  The youths grasp their swords, and for combat prepare;
    While beauty weeps fathers, and lovers, and brothers,
  Who are gone to defend—

—Alas! what a golden, delicious afternoon is blowing without there, wasting for ever; and never a glimpse of it. Delicate work this! Here's a needle might serve for a genuine stiletto! No matter,—it is the cause,—it is the cause that makes, as my mother says, each stitch in this clumsy fabric a grander thing than the flashing of the bravest lance that brave knight ever won.

(Singing)
  The brooks are talking in the dell,
  Tul la lul, tul la lul,
  The brooks are talking low, and sweet,
  Under the boughs where th' arches meet;
  Come to the dell, come to the dell,
  Oh come, come.

  The birds are singing in the dell,
  Wee wee whoo, wee wee whoo;
  The birds are singing wild and free,
  In every bough of the forest tree,
  Come to the dell, come to the dell,

Oh come, come.

And there the idle breezes lie,
Whispering, whispering,
Whispering with the laughing leaves.
And nothing says each idle breeze,
But come, come, come, O lady come,
Come to th' dell.

[*Mrs. Grey enters from without.*]

Mrs. G. Do not sing, Annie.

Annie. Crying would better befit the times, I know,—Dear mother, what is this?

Mrs. G. Hush,—asleep—is she?

Annie. This hour, and quiet as an infant. Need enough there was of it too. See, what a perfect damask mother!

Mrs. G. Draw the curtain on that sunshine there. This sleep has flushed her. Ay, a painter might have dropped that golden hair,—yet this delicate beauty is but the martyr's wreath now, with its fine nerve and shrinking helplessness. No, Annie; put away your hat, my love,—you cannot go to the lodge to-night.

Annie. Mother?

Mrs. G. You cannot go to the glen to-night. This is no time for idle pleasure, God knows.

Annie. Why, you have been weeping in earnest, and your cheek is pale.—And now I know where that sad appointment led you. Is it over? That it should be in our humanity to bear, what in our ease we cannot, *cannot* think of!

Mrs. G. Harder things for humanity are there than bodily anguish, sharp though it be. It was not the boy,—the mother's anguish, I wept for, Annie.

Annie. Poor Endross! And he will go, to his dying day, a crippled thing. But yesterday I saw him springing by so proudly! And the mother—

Mrs. G. "*Words, words,*" she answered sternly when I tried to comfort her; "ay, words are easy. *Wait till you see your own child's blood.* Wait till you stand by and see his young limbs hewn away, and the groans come thicker and thicker that you cannot soothe; and then let them prate to you of the good cause." Bitter words! God knows what is in store for us;—all day this strange dread has clung to me.

Annie. Dear mother, is not this the superstition you were wont to chide?

Mrs. G. Ay, ay, we should have been in Albany ere this. In these wild times, Annie, every chance-blown straw that points at evil, is likely to prove a faithful index; and if it serve to nerve the heart for it, we may call it heaven-sent indeed. Annie,—hear me calmly, my child,—the enemy, so at least goes the rumor, are nearer than we counted on this morning, and—hush, not a word.

Annie. She is but dreaming. Just so she murmured in her sleep last night; twice she waked me with the saddest cry, and after that she sat all night by the window in her dressing-gown, I could not persuade her to sleep again. Tell me, mother, you say *and*—and what?

Mrs. G. I cannot think it true, 'tis rumored though, that these savage neighbors of ours have joined the enemy.

Annie. No! no! Has Alaska turned against us? Why, it was but yesterday I saw him with Leslie in yonder field. 'Tis false; it must be. Surely he could not harm us.

Mrs. G. And false, I trust it is. At least till it is proved otherwise, Helen must not hear of it.

Annie. And why?

Mrs. Grey. She needs no caution, and it were useless to add to the idle fear with which she regards them all, already. Some dark fancy possesses her to-day; I have marked it myself.

Annie. It is just two years to-morrow, mother, since Helen's wedding day, or rather, that sad day that should have seen her bridal; and it cannot be that she has quite forgotten Everard Maitland. Alas, he seemed so noble!

Mrs. G. Hush! Never name him. Your sister is too high-hearted to waste a thought on him. Tory! Helen is no love-lorn damsel, child, to pine for an unworthy love. See the rose on that round cheek,—it might teach that same haughty loyalist, could he see her now, what kind of hearts 'tis that we patriots wear, whose strength they think to trample. Where are you going, Annie?

Annie. Not beyond the orchard-wall. I will only stroll down the path here, just to breathe this lovely air a little; indeed, there's no fear of my going further now.

[*Exit.*

Mrs. G. Did I say right, Helen? It cannot be feigned. Those quick smiles, with their thousand lovely meanings; those eyes, whose beams lead straight to the smiling soul. Principle is it? There is no principle in this, but joy, or else it strikes so deep, that the joy grows up from it, genuine, not feigned; and yet I have found her weeping once or twice of late, in unexplained agony. Helen!

Helen. Oh mother! is it you? Thank God. I thought—

Mrs. G. What did you think? What moves you thus?

Helen. I thought—'tis nothing. This *is* very strange.

Mrs. G. Why do you look through that window thus? There's no one there! What is it that's so strange?

Helen. Is it to-morrow that we go?

Mrs. G. To Albany? Why, no; on Thursday. You are bewildered, Helen! surely you could not have forgotten that.

Helen. I wish it was to-day. I do.

Mrs. G. My child, yesterday, when the question was debated here, and wishing might have been of some avail, 'tis true you did not say much, but I thought, and so we all did, that you chose to stay.

Helen. Did you? Mother, does the road to Albany wind over a hill like that?

Mrs. G. Like what, Helen?

Helen. Like yonder wooded hill, where the soldiers are stationed now?

Mrs. G. Not that I know of? Why?

Helen. Perhaps we may cross that very hill,—no—could we?

Mrs. G. Not unless we should turn refugees, my love; an event of which there is little danger just now, I think. That road, as indeed you know yourself, leads out directly to the British camp.

Helen. Yes—yes—it does. I know it does. I will not yield to it. 'Tis folly, all.

Mrs. G. You talk as though you were dreaming still; my child. Put on your hat, and go into the garden for a little, the air is fresh and pleasant now; or take a ramble through the orchard if you will, you might meet Annie there,—no, yon she comes, and well too. It's quite time that I were gone again. I wish that we had nothing worse than dreams on hand. Helen, I must talk with you about these fancies; you must not thus unnerve yourself for real evil.

[*Exit.*

Helen. It were impossible,—it could not be!—how could it be?—Oh! these are wild times. Unseen powers are crossing their meshes here around us,—and, what am I—Powers?—there's but one Power, and that—
 —"He careth for the little bird,
 Far in the lone wood's depths, and though dark weapons
 And keen eyes are out, it falleth not
 But at his will."

[*Exit.*

PART SECOND

LOVE

DIALOGUE I.

SCENE. *A little glen in the woods near Fort Edward. A young British Officer appears, attended by a soldier in the American uniform; the latter with a small sealed pacquet in his hand.*

Off. Hist!

Sol. Well, so I did; but—

Off. Hist, I say!

Sol. A squirrel it is, Sir; there he sits.

Off. By keeping this path you avoid the picket on the hill. It will bring you out where these woods skirt the vale, and scarcely a hundred rods from the house itself.

[*Calling without.*]

Sol. Captain Andre—Sir.

Off. It were well that the pacquet should fall into no other hands. With a little caution there is no danger. It will be twilight ere you get out of these woods—

Sol. I beg your pardon, Sir; but here is that young Indian guide of mine, after all, above there, beckoning me.

Off. Stay—you will come back to the camp ere midnight?

Sol. Unless some of these quick-eyed rebels see through my disguise.

Off. Do not forget the lodge as you return. A little hut of logs just in the edge of the woods, but Siganaw knows it well.

[*Exit the Soldier.*

(*The call in the thicket above is repeated, and another young officer enters the glen.*)

2nd Off. Hillo, Maitland! These woods yield fairies,—come this way.

1st Off. For God's sake, Andre! (*motioning silence.*) Are you mad?

Andre. Well, who are they?

Mait. Who? Have you forgotten that we are on the enemy's ground? Soldiers from the fort, no doubt. They have crossed that opening twice since we stood here.

Andre. Well, let them cross twice more. I would run the risk of a year's captivity, at least, for one such glimpse. Nay, come, she will be gone.

Mait. Stay,—not yet. There, again!

Andre. Such a villainous scratching as I got in that pass just now. It must have cost the rogues an infinite deal of pains though. A regular, handsome sword-cut is nothing to a dozen of these same ragged scratches, that a man can't swear about. After all, Captain Maitland, these cunning Yankees understand the game. They will keep out of our way, slyly enough, until we are starved, and scratched, and fretted down to their proportions, meanwhile they league the very trees against us.

Mait. As to that, we have made some leagues ourselves, I think, quite as hard to be defended, Sir.

Andre. It may be so. Should we not be at the river by this?

Mait. Sunset was the time appointed. We are as safe here, till then.

Andre. 'Tis a little temple of beauty you have lighted on, in truth. These pretty singers overhead, seem to have no guess at our hostile errand. Methinks their peaceful warble makes too soft a welcome for such warlike comers. Hark! [*Whistling.*] That's American. One might win bloodless laurels here. Will you stand a moment just as you are, Maitland;—'tis the very thing. There's a little space in my unfinished picture, and with that *a la Kemble* mien, you were a fitting mate for this young Dian here, (*taking a pencil sketch from his portfolio,*)—the beauty-breathing, ay, beauty-breathing, it's no poetry;—for the lonesome little glen smiled to its darkest nook with her presence.

Mait. What are you talking of, Andre? Fairies and goddesses!—What next?

Andre. I am glad you grow a little curious at last. Why I say, and your own eyes may make it good if you will, that just down in this glen below here, not a hundred rods hence, there sits, or stands, or did some fifteen minutes since, some creature of these woods, I suppose it is; what else could it be? Well, well, I'll call no names, since they offend you, Sir; but this I'll say, a young cheek and smiling lip it had, whate'er it was, and round and snowy arm, and dimpled hand, that lay ungloved on her sylvan robe, and eyes—I tell you plainly, they lighted all the glen.

Mait. Ha? A lady?—there? Are you in earnest?

Andre. A lady, well you would call her so perchance. Such ladies used to spring from the fairy nut-shells, in the old time, when the kings' son lacked a bride; and if this were Windsor forest that stretches about us here, I might fancy, perchance, some royal one had wandered out, to cool the day's glow in her cheek, and nurse her love-dream; but here, in this untrodden wilderness, unless your ladies here spring up like flowers, or drop down on invisible pinions from above, how, in the name of reason, came she here?

Mait. On the invisible pinions of thine own lady-loving fancy; none otherwise, trust me.

Andre. Come, come,—see for yourself. On my word I was a little startled though, as my eye first lighted on her, suddenly, in that lonesome spot. There she sat, so bright and still, like some creature of the leaves and waters, such as the old Greeks fabled, that my first thought was to worship her; my next—of you, but I could not leave the spot until I had sketched this; I stood unseen, within a yard of her; for I could see her soft breath stirring the while. See, the scene itself was a picture,—the dark glen, the lonesome little lodge, on the very margin of the fairy lake—here she sat, motionless as marble; this bunch of roses had dropped from her listless hand, and you would have thought some tragedy of ancient sorrow, were passing before her, in the invisible element, with such a fixed and lofty sadness she gazed into it. But of course, of course, it is nothing to *your* eye; for me, it will serve to bring the whole out at my leisure. Indeed, the air, I think, I have caught a little as it is.

Mait. A little—you may say it. She is there, is she?—sorrowful; well, what is't to me?

Andre. What do you say?—There?—Yes, I left her there at least. Come, come. I'll show you one will teach you to unlearn this fixed contempt of gentle woman. Come.

Mait. Let go, if you please, Sir. She who gave me my first lesson in that art, is scarcely the one to bid me now unlearn it, and I want no new teaching as yet, thank Heaven. Will you come? We have loitered here long enough, I think.

Andre. What, under the blue scope—what the devil ails you, Maitland?

Mait. Nothing, nothing. This much I'll say to you, —*that lady is my wife*.

Andre. Nonsense!

Mait. There lacked—three days, I think it was, three whole days, to the time when the law would have given her that name; but for all that, was she mine, and is; Heaven and earth cannot undo it.

Andre. Are you in earnest? Why, are we not here in the very heart of a most savage wilderness, where never foot of man trod before,—unless you call these wild red creatures men?

Mait. You talk wildly; that path, followed a few rods further, would have brought you out within sight of her mother's door.

Andre. Ha! you have been in this wilderness then, ere now?

Mait. Have you forgotten the fortune I wasted once on a summer's seat, some few miles up, on the lake above? These Yankees did me the grace to burn it, just as the war broke out.

Andre. Ay, ay, that was *here*. I had forgotten the whereabouts. Those blackened ruins we passed last evening, perchance;—and the lady—my wood-nymph, what of her?

Mait. Captain Andre, I beg your pardon, Sir. That sketch of yours reminded me, by chance perhaps, of one with whom some painful passages of my life are linked; and I said, in my haste, what were better left unsaid. Do me the favor not to remind me that I have done so.

Andre. So—so! And I am to know nothing more of this smiling apparition; nay, not so much as to speak her name? Consider, Maitland, I am your friend it is true; but, prithee, consider the human in me. Give her a local habitation, or at least a name.

Mait. I have told you already that the lady you speak of resides not far hence. On the border of these woods you may see her home. I may point it out to you securely, some few days hence;—to-night, unless you would find yourself in the midst of the American army, this must content you.

Andre. A wild risk for a creature like that! Have these Americans no safer place to bestow their daughters than the fastnesses of this wilderness?

Mait. It would seem so. Yet it is her home. Wild as it looks here, from the top of that hill, where our men came out on the picket just now so suddenly, you will see as fair a picture of cultured life as e'er your eyes looked on. No English horizon frames a lovelier one.

Andre. Here? No!

Mait. Between that hill and the fort, there stretches a wide and beautiful plain, covered with orchards and meadows to the wood's edge; and here and there a gentle swell, crowned with trees, some patch of the old wilderness. The infant Hudson winds through it, circling in its deepest bend one little fairy isle, with woods enough for a single bower, and a beauty that fills and characterizes, to its remotest line, the varied landscape it centres; and far away in the east, this same azure mountain-chain we have traced so long, with its changeful light and shade, finishes the scene.

Andre. You should have been a painter, Maitland.

Mait. The first time I beheld it—one summer evening it was, from the woods on the hill's brow;—we were a hunting party, I had lost my way, and ere I knew it there I stood;—its waters lay glittering in the sunset light, and the window-panes of its quiet dwellings were flashing like gold,—the old brown houses looked out through the trees like so many lighted palaces; and even the little hut of logs, nestling on the wood's edge, borrowed beauty from the hour. I was miles from home; but the setting sun could not warn me away from such a paradise, for so it seemed, set in that howling wilderness, and—

Andre. Prithee, go on. I listen.

Mait. I know not how it was, but as I wandered slowly down the shady road, for the first time in years of worldliness, the dream that had haunted my boyhood revived again. Do you know what I mean, Andre?—that dim yearning for lovelier beings and fairer places, whose ideals lie in the heaven-fitted mind, but not in the wilderness it wakes in; that mystery of our nature, that overlooked as it is, and trampled with unmeaning things so soon, hides, after all, the whole secret of this life's dark enigma.

Andre. But see,—our time is well-nigh gone,—this is philosophy—I would have heard a love tale.

Mait. It was then, that near me, suddenly I heard the voice that made this dull, real world, thenceforth a richer place for me than the gorgeous dream-land of childhood was of old.

Andre. Ay, ay—go on.

Mait. Andre, did you ever meet an eye, in which the intelligence of our nature idealized, as it were, the very poetry of human thought seemed to look forth?

Andre. One such.

Mait.—That reflected your whole being; nay, revealed from its mysterious depths, new consciousness, that yet seemed like a faint memory, the traces of some old and pleasant dream?

Andre. Methinks the heavenly revelation itself doth that.

Mait. Such an eye I saw then shining on me. A clump of stately pines grew on the sloping road-side, and, looking into its dark embrasure, I beheld a group of merry children around a spring that gurgled out of the hillside there, and among them, there sat a young girl clad in white, her hat on the bank beside her, tying a wreath of wild flowers. That was all—that was all, Andre.

Andre. Well, she was beautiful, I suppose? Nay, if it was the damsel I met just now I need not ask.

Mait. Beautiful? Ay, they called her so. *Beauty* I had seen before; but from that hour the sun shone with another light, and the very dust and stones of this dull earth were precious to me. *Beautiful?* Nay, it was *she.* I knew her in an instant, the spirit of my being; she whose existence made the lovely whole, of which mine alone had been the worthless and despised fragment. There are a thousand women on the earth the artist might call as lovely,—show me another that I can worship.

Andre. Worship! This is Captain Everard Maitland. If I should shut my eyes now—

Mait. Well, go on; but I tell you, ne'ertheless, there have been times, even in this very spot,—we often wandered here when the day was dying as it is now,—here in her soft, breathing loveliness, she has stood beside me, when I have,—*worshipped?*—nay, feared her, in her holy beauty, as we two should an angel who should come through that glade to us now.

Andre. True it is, something of the Divinity there is in beauty, that, in its intenser forms, repels with all its winningness, until the lowliness of love looks through it. Well—you worshipped her.

Mait. Nay, you have told the rest. I would have worshipped; but one day there came a look from those beautiful eyes, when I met them suddenly, with a gaze that sought the mystery of their beauty,—a single look, and in an instant the drooping lash had buried it forever; but I knew, ere it fell, that the world of her young being was all mine already. Another life had been forever added unto mine; a whole creation; yet, like Eden's fairest, it but made another perfect; a new and purer *self;* and in it grew the heaven, and the fairy-land of my old dreams, lovelier than ever. You have loved yourself, Andre, else I should weary you.

Andre. Not a bit the more do I understand you though. You talk most lover-like; that's very clear, yet I must say I never saw the part worse played. Why, here's your ladye-love, this self-same idol of whom you rave, at this moment perchance, breathing within these woods,—years too—two mortal years it must be, since you have seen her face; and yet—you stand here yet, with folded arms;—a goodly lover, on my word!

Mait. Softly, Sir! you grace me with a title to which I can lay no claim. Lover I *was*, may be. I am no lover now, not I—not I; you are right; I would not walk to that knoll's edge to see the lady, Sir.

Andre. Well, I must wait your leisure, I see.

Mait. And yet, the last time that we stood together here, her arm lay on mine, my promised wife. A few days more, and by *my* name, all that loveliness had gone. There needed only that to make that tie holy in all eyes, the holiest which the universe held for us; but needed there that, or any thing to make it such in ours. Why, love lay in her eye, that evening, like religion, solemn and calm.—We should have smiled then at the thought of any thing in height or depth, ending, what through each instant seemed to breathe eternity from its own essence;—we were one, *one,*—that trite word makes no meaning in your ear.—to me, life's roses burst from it; music, sunshine, Araby, should image what it means; what it meant rather, for it is over.

Andre. What was it, Maitland?

Mail. Oh,—well,—she did not love me; that was all. So far my story has told the seeming only, but ere long the trial came, and then I found it *was* seeming, in good sooth. The Rebellion had then long been maturing, as you know; but just then came the crisis. It was the one theme everywhere. Of course I took my king's part against these rebels, and at once I was outraged, wronged beyond all human bearing. Her mad brother, her's, *her's* what a world of preciousness, Andre, that little word once enshrined for me; and still it seems like some broken vase, fragrant with what it held.

Andre. And ever with that name, a rosy flash Paints, for an instant, all my world. Nay, 'tis a little love-poem of my own; go on, Maitland.

Mait. This brother I say, quarrelled with me, though I had borne from him unresentingly, what from another would have seemed insult. We quarrelled at last, and the house was closed against me, or would have been had I sought access; for I walked sternly by its pleasant door that afternoon, though I remember now how the very roses that o'erhung the porch, the benched and shaded porch, that lovely lingering place, seemed to beckon me in. It was a breathless summer day, and the vine curled in the open window,—even now those lowly rooms make a brighter image of heaven to me than the jewelled walls that of old grew in the pageant of our sabbath dreams.

Andre. And thus you abandoned your love? A quarrel with her brother?

Mait. I never wronged her with the shadow of a doubt. Directly, that same day, I wrote to her to fix our meeting elsewhere, that we might renew our broken plans in some fitter shape for the altered times. She sent me a few lines of grave refusal, Sir; and the next letter was returned unopened.

Andre. 'Twas that brother! Pshaw! 'twas that brother, Maitland. I'll lay my life the lady saw no word of it.

Mait. I might have thought so too, perchance; but that same day,—the morning had brought the news from Boston,—I met her by chance, by the spring in the little grove where we first met; and—Good Heavens! she talked of brothers! Brothers, mother, sisters!—What was their right to mine? All that the round world holds, or the universe, what could it be to her?—that is, if she had loved me ever; which, past all doubt, she never did.

Andre. Maitland! Heavens, how this passion blinds you! And you expected a gentle, timid girl like that to abandon all she loved. Nay, to make her home in the very camp, where death and ruin unto all she loved, was the watchword?

Mait. I beg your pardon, Sir. I looked for no such thing. I offered to renounce my hopes of honor here for her; a whole life's plans, for her sake I counted nothing. I offered her a home in England too, the very real of her girlhood's wish; my blighted fortunes since, or a home in yonder camp,—never, never. But if I had, ay, if I had,—that is not *love*, call it what you will, it is not love, to which such barriers were any thing.

Andre. Oh well, a word's a word. That's as one likes. Only with your definition, give me leave to say, marvellous little love, Captain Maitland, marvellous little you will find in this poor world of ours.

Mait. I'll grant ye.

Andre. If there is any thing like it outside of a poet's skull, ne'er credit me.

Mait. Strange it should take such shape in the creating thought and in the yearning heart, when all reality hath not its archetype.

Andre. Hist!

Mait. A careful step,—one of our party I fancy.

Andre. 'Tis time we were at the rendezvous. If we have to recross the river as we came, on the stumps of that old bridge, we had best keep a little day-light with us, I think.

[*Exeunt.*

DIALOGUE II.

SCENE. *A chamber in the Parsonage. Helen leaning from the open window.*

(*Annie enters.*)

Annie. Helen Grey, where on earth have you been? *Wood flowers!*

Helen. Come and look at this sunset.

Annie. Surely you have not, you cannot have been in those woods, Helen: and yet, where else could this periwinkle grow, and these wild roses?—Delicious!

Helen. Hear that flute. It comes from among those trees by the river side.

Annie. It is the shower that has freshened every thing, and made the birds so musical. You should stand in the door below, as I did just now, to see the fort and the moistened woods stands out from that black sky, with all this brightness blazing on them.

Helen. 'Tis lovely—all.

Annie. There goes the last golden rim over the blackening woods; already even a shade of tender mourning steals over all things, the very children's voices under this tree,—how soft they grow.

Helen. Will the day come when we shall see him sink, for the last time, behind those hills?

Annie. Nay, Helen, why do you mar this lovely hour with a thought like that?

Helen. And in another life, shall we see light, when his, for us, shines no more?—What sound is that?

Annie. That faint cry from the woods?

Helen. No,—more distant,—far off as the horizon, like some mighty murmur, faintly borne, it came.

Annie. I wish that we had gone to-day. I do not like this waiting until Thursday;—just one of that elder brother's foolish whims it was. I cannot think how your consent was won to it. Did you meet any one in your walk just now?

Helen. No—Yes, yes, I did. The little people where I went, I met by hundreds, Annie. Through the dark aisles, and the high arches, all decked in blue, and gold, and crimson, they sung me a most merry welcome. And such as these—see—You cannot think how like long-forgotten friends they looked, smiling up from their dark homes, upon me.

Annie. You have had chance enough to forget them, indeed,—it is two years, Helen, since you have been in those woods before. What could have tempted you there to-day?

Helen. Was there *danger* then?—was there danger indeed?—I was by the wood-side ere I knew it, and then,—it was but one last look I thought to take—nay, what is it, Annie? George met me as I was coming home, and I remember something in his eye startled me at first; but if there was danger, I should have known of it before.

Annie. How could we dream of your going there this evening, when we knew you had never set your foot in those woods since the day Everard Maitland left Fort Edward?

Helen. Annie!

Annie. For me, I would as soon have looked to see Maitland himself coming from those woods, as you.

Helen. Annie! Annie Grey! You must not, my sister—do not speak that name to me, never again, *never*.

Annie. Why, Helen, I am sorry to have grieved you thus; but I thought—Look! look! There go those officers again,—there, in the lane between the orchards, Scarcely half an hour ago they went by to the fort in just such haste. There is something going on there, I am sure.

(*Helen rises from the window, and walks the room.*)

Annie. In truth there was a rumor this afternoon,—you are so timid and fanciful, our mother chose you should not hear it while it was rumor only; but 'tis said that a party of the enemy have been seen in those woods to-day, and, among them, the Indians we have counted so friendly. Do you hear me, Helen?

Helen. That he should *live* still! Yes, it is all real still! That heaven of my thought, that grows so like a pageant to me, is still *real* somewhere. Those eyes—they are darkly shining now; this very moment that passes *me*, drinks their beauty;—that voice,—that tone,—that very tone—on some careless ear, even now it wastes its luxury of blessing. Continents of hail and darkness, the polar seas—all earth's distance, could never have parted me from him; but now I live in the same world with him, and the everlasting walls blacken between us. Those looks may shine on the dull earth and senseless stones, but not on me; on uncaring eyes, but not on mine; though for one moment of their lavished wealth, I could cheaply give a life without them; never again, never, never, never shall their love come to me.

Annie. Who would have thought she could cherish in secret a grief like this? Dear sister, we all believed you had forgotten that sad affair long ago,—we thought that you were happy now.

Helen. Happy?—I am, you were right; but I have been to-day down to the very glen where we took that last lovely walk together, and all the beautiful past came back to me like life.—I *am* happy; you must count me so still.

Annie. With what I have just now heard, how can I?

Helen. It is this war that has parted us; and so, this is but my part in these noble and suffering times, and that great thought reaches overall my anguish. But for this war I might have been—hath this world such flowers, and do they call it a wilderness?—I might have been, even now, you know it, Annie, his wife, his wife, *his*. But our hearts are cunningly made, many-stringed; and often much good music is left in them when we count them broken. That which makes the bitterness of this lot, the inconceivable, unutterable bitterness of it, even that I can bear now, calmly, and count it God's kindness too.

Annie. I do not understand you, sister.

Helen. What if this young royalist, Annie, when he quarrelled with my brother, and took arms against my country, what if he had kept faith to *me?*

Annie. Well.

Helen. Well? Oh no, it would not have been well. Why, my home would have been with that pursuing army now, my fate bound up with that hollow cause,—these very hands might have fastened the sword of oppression; nay, the sword whose edge was turned against you, against you all, and against the cause, that with tears, night and morning, you were praying for, and with your heart's best blood stood ready to seal every hour. No, it is best as it is; or if my wish grows deeper still, if in my heart I envy, with murmuring thought, the blessed brides, on whose wedding dawns the laughing sun of peace, then with a wish I cast away the glory of these suffering times.—It is best as it is. I am content.

Annie. I wish I could understand you, Helen. You say, "if he had kept faith to you;"—carried you off, you mean! Do you mean, sister Helen, that of your own will you would ever have gone with him, with Everard Maitland,—that traitor?

Helen. Gone with him? Would I not? Would I not? Dear child, we talk of what, as yet, you know nothing of. Gone with *him?* Some things are holy, Annie, only until the holier come.

Annie. (*looking toward the door.*) Stay, stay. What is it, George?

(*George Grey comes in.*)

George. I was seeking our mother. What should it be, but ill news? This tide is against us, and if it be not well-nigh full, we may e'en fold our arms for the rest. There, read that. (*Throwing her a letter.*)

Every face you see looks as if a thunder-cloud were passing it. I heard one man say, just now, as I came in, that the war would be over in a fortnight's time. There'll be some blood spilt ere then, I reckon though.

Helen. What paper is that that reddens her cheek so suddenly?

Annie. The McGregor's!—think of it, Helen,—gone over to the British side, and St. John of the Glens, and—who brought you this letter, George? 'Tis false! I do not believe it, not a word of it. Why, here are twenty names, people that we know, the most honorable, too,—forsaking us now, at such a crisis!

George. Self-defence, self-defence, sister; their lands and their houses must be saved from devastation. What sort of barracks think you, would that fine country-seat of McGregor's make?—and St. John's—*he* is a farmer you know, and his fields are covered with beautiful grain, that a week will ripen, and so, he is for turning his sword into a sickle;—besides, there are worse things than pillage threatened here. Look, (*unfolding a hand-bill.*) Just at this time comes this villainous proclamation from Skeensborough, scattered about among our soldiers nobody knows how, half of them on the eve of desertion before, and the other half—what ails you, Helen?

Helen. There he stands!

Annie. Is she crazed? Why do you clasp your hands so wildly? for Heaven's sake, Helen!—her cheek is white as death.—Helen!

Helen. Is he gone, Annie?

Annie. As I live, I do not know what you are talking of. Nay, look; there is no one here, none that you need fear, most certainly.

Helen. I saw him, his eye was on me; there he stood, looking through that window, smiling and beckoning me.

George. Saw him? Who, in Heaven's name? This is fancy-work.

Helen. I saw him as I see you now. He stood on that roof,—an Indian,—I saw the crimson bars on his face, and the blanket, and the long wild hair on his shoulders; and—and, I saw the gleaming knife in his girdle,—Oh God! I did.

George. Ay, ay, 'twas that scoundrel that dogged us in our way home, I'll lay my life it was.

Helen. In our way home? An *Indian*, I said.

George. Well, well, and I say an Indian, a rascal Indian, was watching and following us all the way home just now.

Helen. George!

George. Then you did not see him after all. In truth, I did not mean you should, for we could not have hurried more, but all the time we sat in that shanty, while it rained, about as far off as that chair from me, stood this same fellow among the bushes, watching us, or rather you. And you saw him here t He might have crept along by that orchard wall. What are you laughing at, Annie?—I will go and see what sort of a guard we have.

Annie. If you knew as much of Helen's Indians as I do, you would hardly be in such a hurry, George, I mean about this one that was here just now, for there are Indians in yonder forest I suppose; but since we were so high, I never walked in the woods with her once, but that we encountered one, or heard his steps among the bushes at least; and if it chanced to be as late as this, there would be half a dozen of them way laying us in the road,—but sometimes they turned out squirrels, and sometimes logs of wood, and sometimes mere air, air of about this color. We want a little light, that is all. There is no weapon like that for these fancy-people. I can slay a dozen of them with a candle's beams.

(*George goes out.*)

Helen. Do not laugh at me to-night, Annie.

Annie. But what should the Indians want of you, pry'thee; tell me that, Helen?

Helen. God knows. Wait till the sun sets to-morrow, and I will laugh with you if you are merry then.

Annie. Why to-morrow?—because it is our last day here? Tuesday—Wednesday—yes; the next day we shall be on the road to Albany.

[*Exit.*

Helen. I am awake now. Watched me in the glen?—followed me home? Those woods are full of them.—But what has turned their wild eyes on me?

It is but one day longer;—we have counted many, in peril and fear, and *this*, is the last;—even now how softly the fearful time wastes. *One day!*—Oh God, thou only knowest what its shining walls encircle. (*She leans on the window, musing silently*.) Two years ago I stood here, and prayed to die.-On that same tree my eye rested then. With what visions of hope I played under it once, building bowers for fairies I verily thought would come, and dreaming, with yearning heart, of glorious and beautiful things this world *hath not*. But, that wretched day, through blinding tears, I saw the sunlight on its glossy leaves, and I said, 'let me see that light no more.' Surely the bitterness is deep when that which hath colored all our unfolded being, is a weariness. For what more hath life for me I thought, its lesson is learned and its power is spent,—it can please, and it can trouble me no more; and why should I stay here in vain and wearily?

It was sad enough, indeed, to see the laughing spring returning again, when the everlasting winter had set in within, to link with each change of the varied year, sweet with a life's memories, such mournfulness; laying by, one by one, all hope's blessed spells, withered and broken forever,—the moonlight, the songs of birds, the blossom showers of April, the green and gold of autumn's sunset,—it was sad, but it was not in vain.—Not in vain, Oh God, didst thou deny that weeping prayer.

(*A merry voice is heard without, and a child's face peeps through the window that overlooks the orchard.*)

Child. Look! look! sister Helen! see what I have found on the roof of the piazza here,—all covered with wampum and scarlet, and here are feathers too—two feathers in it, blue and yellow—eagle's feathers they are, I guess.

Helen (*approaching the window.*) Let me see, Willy. What, did you find it here?

Willy. Just under the window here. Frank and I were swinging on the gate; and—there is something hard in it, Helen,—feel.

Helen. Yes, it is very curious; but—

Willy. There comes Netty with the candle; now we can see to untie this knot.

Helen. Willy, dear Willy, you must give it to me, you must indeed, and—I will paint you a bird to-morrow.

Willy. A blue-bird, will you? A real one?

Helen. Yes, yes;—run down little climber; see how dark it grows, and Frank is waiting, see.

Willy. Well. But mind you, it must be a blue bird then. A real one. With the red on his breast, and all.

[*Exit.*

(*She walks to the table, unfastening the envelope.*)

Helen. What sent that thrill of forgotten life through me then?—that wild, delicious thrill? This is strange, indeed. A sealed pacquet within! and here—

(*She glances at the superscription, and the pacquet drops from her hand.*)

No—no. I have seen that hand-writing in my dreams before, but it dissolved always. What's joy better than grief, if it pierce thus? Can never a one of all the soul's deep melodies on this poor instrument be played out, then —trembling and jarring thus, even at the breath of its most lovely passion.—And yet, it is some cruel thing, I know.

(*The pacquet opened, discovers Helen's miniature, a book, a ring, and other tokens.*)

Cruel indeed! That little rose!—He might have spared me this. A dull reader I were, in truth, if this needed comment,—but I knew it before. He might have spared me this.

(*She leans over the recovered relics with a burst of passionate weeping.*)

Yet, who knows—(*lifting her head with a sudden smile,*) some trace, some little curl of his pencil I may find among these leaves yet, to tell me, as of old,—

(*A letter drops from the book, she tears it eagerly open.*)

(*Reading.*) These cold words I understand, but—*letters!*—He wrote me none! Was there ever a word between us, from the hour when he left me, his fancied bride, to that last meeting, when, at a word, and ere I knew what I had said, he turned on me that cold and careless eye, and left me, haughtily and forever? And now—(*reading*)—misapprehension, has it been! Is the sun on high again?—in this black and starless night—the noonday sun? He loves me still.—Oh! this joy weighs like grief.

Shall I see him again? Joy! joy! Beautiful sunshine joy! Who knows the soul's rich depths till joy hath lighted them?—from the dim and sorrowful haunts of memory will he come again into the living present! Shall I see those eyes, looking on me? Shall I hear my name in that lost music sound once more?—His?—Am I his again? New mantled with that shining love, like some glorious and beautiful stranger I seem to myself, *Helen*—the bright and joy-wreathed thing his voice makes that name mean— My life will be all full of that blest music. I shall be Helen, evermore his—his.

No,—it would make liars of old sages,—and all books would read wrong. A life of such wild blessedness? It would be fearful like living in some magic land, where the honest laws of nature were not. A life?—a moment were enough. Ages of common life would shine in it. (*Reading again.*) "Elliston's hut?"—"If I choose that the return should be mutual,—and the memorials of a despised regard can at best be but an indifferent possession;—a pacquet reinclosed directly in this same envelope, and left at the hut of the missionary, cannot fail to reach him safely."

"Safely."—Might he not come there safely then? And might I not go thither safely too, in to-morrow's light?

O God, let not Passion lead me now. The centre beaming truth, not passion's narrow ray, must light me here!—But am I not his?

Once more, one horizon circles, for a day, our long-parted destinies; another, and another wave of these wild times will drift them asunder again, forever; and I count myself his wife. His wife?—nay, his bride, his two years' bride, to-night, his wife, to-morrow. He must meet me there, (*writing*) at noon, I will say.—I did not think that little hut of logs should have been my marriage-hall;—he must meet me there, and to-morrow is my bridal day.

PART THIRD.

FATE.

DIALOGUE I.

SCENE. *The hill—Night—Large fires burning—Sentinels dimly seen in the back-ground. A young Indian steals carefully from the thicket. He examines the ground and the newly-felled trees.*

Indian. One, two, three. And this is ringed. The dogs have spoiled the council-house.

(*Soldiers rush forward.*)

1st Sol. So, Mr. Red-skin! would not you like a scalp or two now, to string on your leggings? Maybe we can help you to one or so. Hold fast. Take care of that arm, I know him of old.

(*The Indian, with a violent struggle, disengages himself, and darts into the thicket.*)

No? well,—dead or alive, we must have you on our side again. (*Firing.*)

2nd Sol. He's fixed, Sir.

1st Sol. Hark. Hark,—off again! Let me go. What do you hold me for, you scoundrel?

2nd Sol. Don't make a fool of yourself, Will Wilson. There will be a dozen of them yelling around you there. Besides, he is half way to the swamp by this. Look here; what's this, in the grass here?

1st Sol. There was something in his hand, but he clenched it through it all,—this is a letter. Bring it to the fire.

2nd Sol. (*reading.*) "*This by the Indian, as in case I am taken, he may reach the camp in safety. Not over three thousand men in all, I should think,—very little ammunition, soldiers mostly discouraged.—In Albany, they are tearing the lead off the windows of the houses, and taking the weights from the shops for ball. Talk of retreating on Thursday to the new encampment, five miles below. More when I get to you.*"

More! Humph! A pretty string of lies he has got here already. This must go to the General, Dick.

[*Exeunt.*

DIALOGUE II.

SCENE. *Chamber in the Parsonage. Moonlight. Annie sitting by the window, the door open into an adjoining room.*

Annie. (*Calling.*) Come, come,—why do you sit there scribbling so late, Helen? Come, and enjoy this beautiful night with me. Ay, what a world of invisible life amid the dew and darkness utters its glad voices; even the little insect we never saw by day, makes us feel for once the great brotherhood of being. This day week we shall be in Albany,—no more such scenes as this then.

(*Helen approaches the window, and puts her arm gently around her sister.*)

Helen. No more!—It was a sad word you were saying, Annie.

Annie. How you startled me. Your hands are cold,—cold as icicles, and trembling too. What ails you, Helen?

Helen. 'Tis nothing.—How often you and I have stood together thus, looking down on that old bridge.—Summer and winter.—Do you remember the cold snowy moonlights of old, when the sound of the distant bell had hope in it? We shall stand together thus, no more.

Annie. Do not speak so sadly, Helen. I cannot think they will destroy our home in mere wantonness. Was there not some one coming up the path just now? Hark! there is news with that tone.

[*Exit.*

Helen. A little more, an hour perchance, and he will read my letter. Why do I tremble thus? Is it because I have done wrong, that these dark misgivings haunt me? No,—it is not remorse—'tis very like—yet remorse it is not. Danger, there is none. I shall but walk to the wood-side as to-day, that little path to the hut is quickly trod, and he will be waiting there. I shall be safe then, safe as I care to be.—Why do I stand here reasoning thus? Safe? And if I were not, what is it to me now? The dark plan is laid. The fearful acting now is all that's left for me.

This must go to the lodge to-night, and ere my mother returns;—to tell them now, would be to make my scheme impossible.

(*She begins, with a reluctant air, to fold the dresses, which are lying loosely by her.*)

Oh God! whence do these dark and horrible thoughts grow?—Nay, feeling not born of thought. That wedding robe looks like a shroud to me! I cannot. Shadows from things unseen are upon me. The future is a night of tempest, where I hear nothing but the breaking boughs, and the whirl and crash of the mourning blast. Oh God! there is no refuge for the fearful, but in thee.—To thee—no. If there is power in prayer of mine, hath it not already doomed that wicked cause, my fate is linked with now. I cannot pray.—Can I not?—How the pure strength comes welling up from its infinite depths.

Hear me—not with lip service, I beseech thee now, but with the earnestness that stays the rushing heart's blood in its way.—Hear me. Let the high cause of right and freedom, whose sad banner, now, on yonder hill, floats in this summer air; whose music on this soft night-breeze is borne—let it prevail—though *I*, with all this sensitive, warm, shrinking life; with all this new-found wealth of love and hope, lie on its iron way.

I am safe now.—This life that I feel now, steel cannot reach.

(*Annie enters.*)

Annie. Dear Helen, dress yourself. It is all true! We must go to-night, we must indeed. They are dismantling the fort now.—Come to the door, and you can hear them if you will; and here is word from Henry, we must be ready before morning—the British are within sight. Do you hear me, Helen? Do not stand looking at me in that strange way.

Helen. To-night!

Annie. I was frightened myself at first, sadly; but there is no danger, not the least. We shall be in Albany to-morrow, Henry says. Come, Helen, there is no one to see to any thing but ourselves. They are running about like mad creatures there below, and the children, are crying, and such a time you never saw.

Helen. To-night! That those beautiful lips should speak it! Take it back. It cannot be. It must not be.

Annie. Why do you look so reproachfully at me? Helen, you astonish and frighten me!

Helen. Yes—yes—I see it all. And why could I not have known this one hour sooner?—Even now it may not be too late. Annie—

Annie. Thank Heaven,—there is my mother's voice at last.

Helen. Annie, stay. Do not mark what I have said in the bewilderment of this sudden fear. Is George below?—Who brought this news?

Annie. One of the men from the fort.—George has not been home since you sent him to Elliston's. She is calling me. Make haste and come down, Helen.

[*Exit.*

Helen. They will leave me alone. They will leave me here alone. And why could I not have known this one hour sooner?—I could have bid him come to-night—If the invisible powers are plotting against me, it is well. Could I have thought of this?—and yet, how like something I had known before, it all comes upon me.—Can I stay here alone?—Could I?—No never, never! He must come for me to-night. Perchance that pacquet still lies at yonder hut, and it is not yet too late to recal my letter;—if it is—if it is, I must find some other messenger. Thank God!—there is one way. Elliston can send to that camp to-night. He can—even now,—He can—he will.—

[*Exit.*

DIALOGUE III.

SCENE. *The porch. Helen waiting the return of her messenger from the hut.*

Helen. How quiet and soft it all lies in this solemn light. Is it illusion?—can it be?—that old, familiar look, that from these woods and hills, and from this moon-lit meadow, seems to smile on me now with such a holy promise of protection and love?—The merry trill in this apple-tree is the very sound that, waking from my infant sleep in the hush of the summer midnight, of old lulled, nay, wakened my first inward thought. Oh that my heart's youngest religion could come again, the feeling with which a little child looks up to these mighty stars, as the spangles on his home-roof, while he stands smiling beneath the awful shelter of the skies, as under a father's dome. But these years show us the evil that mocks that trust.

'Tis he,—What a mere thread of time separates me from my fate, and yet the darkness of ages could not hide it more surely. Already he has reached the lane. Another minute will show me all. Will the pacquet be in his hand, or will it not? I will be calm—it shall be like a picture to me.

Ah! there is an immeasurable power about us, a foreign and strange thing, that answers not to the soul, that seems to know or to heed nothing of the living suffering, rejoicing being of the spirit. Why should I struggle with it any longer? From my weeping childhood to this hour, it hath set its iron bars about me; no—softly yielding, hath it not sometimes, the long, undreamed-of vistas opened, bright as heaven,—and now, maybe—how slow he moves—even now perchance.—This is wrong. The Infinite is One. The Goodness Infinite, whose everlasting smile lighteth the inner soul, and the Power Infinite, whose alien touch without, in darkness comes, they are of One, and the good know it.

The Messenger. (Coming up the path.)

Bless you, Miss! The pacquet had been gone this hour!

Helen. Gone! Well.—And Elliston—what said he?

Mess. I brought this note of yours back, Miss Helen. Father Elliston was gone. Here has been an Indian killed on Sandy Hill this evening, Alaska's own son as it turns out, and such a hubbub as they are making about it you never heard. I met a couple of squaws myself, yelling like mad creatures, and the woods are all alive with them. The priest has gone down to their village to pacify them if it may be,—so I brought the note back, Miss Helen, for there was no one there but a little rascal of an Indian, and I would not trust the worth of a feather with one of them. Was I right?

Helen. Yes. Give it to me. How far is it to the British camp?

Mess. Why, they are just above here at Brandon's Mills they say, that is, the main body. It can't be over three miles, or so.

Helen. Three miles! only three miles of this lovely moonlight road between us.—William McReady, go to that camp for me to-night.

Mess. To the British camp?

Helen. Ay.

Mess. To the British camp! Lord bless you, Miss. I should be shot—I should be shot as true as you are a living woman. I should be shot for a deserter, or, what's worse, I should be hanged for a spy.

Helen. What shall I do!

Mess. And besides, there's Madame Grey will be wanting me by this time. See how the candles dance about the rooms there.

Helen. Yes, you are right. We must go in and help them. Come.

(*They enter the house.*)

DIALOGUE IV.

SCENE. *The British camp. Moonlight. A lady in a rich travelling dress, standing in the door of a log-hut.*

Lady Ackland. (*Talking to her maid within.*) What is the matter, Margaret? What do you go stealing about the walls so like a mad woman for, with that shoe in your hand?

Maid. (*Within.*) There, Sir!—your song is done!—there's one less, I am certain of that. *Coming to the door.*) If ever I get home alive, my lady—Ha!—(*striking the door with her slipper.*) If ever—you are there, are you? I believe I have broken my ear in two. The matter? Will your ladyship look here?

Lady A. Well.

Maid. And if ever I get back to London, I'll say well too. If ever I get back to London alive, my lady,—I'll see—

Lady A. What will you see, Margaret? Nothing lovelier than this, I am sure. Are you not ashamed to stand muttering there? Come here, and look at this beautiful night.

Maid. La, Lady Harriet!

Lady A. Listen! How still the camp is now! You can hear the rush of those falls we passed, distinctly. How pretty the tents look there, in that deep shade. These tuneful frogs and katy-dids must be our nightingales to-night. Indeed, as I stand now, I could almost fancy that fine wood there was my father's park; nay, methinks I see the top of the old gray turrets peeping out among the shadows there. Look, Margaret, do you see?

Maid. La! I can see woods enough, my lady, if that is what you mean,—nothing else, and I have seen enough of them already to last me one life through. Yes, here's a pretty tear I have got amongst them!—Two guineas and a half it cost me in London,—I pray I may never set my eyes on a wood again,

Lady A. This was some happy home once, I know. See that rose-bush, and this little bed of flowers.—Here was a pretty yard—there went the fence,—and there, where that waggon stands, by that broken pear-tree, swung the gate. And pleasant meetings there have been at this door, no doubt, and sorrowful partings too,—and hearts within have leaped at the sound of that gate, and merry tales have been told by that desolate hearth. In this little lonely unthought-of place, the mysterious world of the human soul has unfolded,—the drama of life been played, as grandly in the eyes of angels as in the proud halls where my life dawned. And there are hearts that cling to this desolate spot as mine does to that far-off home. We have driven them away in sorrow and fear. This is war!

Maid. I wonder who is fluting under that tree there, so late. They are serenading that Dutch woman, as I live.

Lady A. The Baroness, are you talking of, Margaret?

Maid. A baroness! Good sooth!—she looks like it, in that yellow silk, and those odious beads, fussing about. If your ladyship will believe me, I saw her sitting in her tent to-night, ay, in the door, feeding that wretched child with her own hands. We can't be thankful enough they did not put her in here with us, I'll own.

Lady A. Hush, hush, for shame! We might well have spared that empty room. Come, we'll go in—It's very late. Strange that Sir George should not be here ere this.

Maid. Look, my lady! Here's some one at the gate.

(*An officer enters the little court, with a hasty step.*)

Officer. Good evening to your ladyship.—Is Captain Maitland here?—Sir George told me that he left him here.

Lady A. Ay, but he has been gone this hour. Stay, it is Andre's flute you hear below there, and some one has joined him just now—yes, it is he.

Off. Under that tree;—thank you, my lady.

Lady A. Stay, Colonel Hill,—I beg your pardon, but you spoke so hastily.—This young Maitland is a friend of ours, I trust there is nothing that concerns him painfully.—

Off. Oh nothing, nothing, except that he is ordered off to Fort Ann to-night. There are none of us that know these wild routes as well as he.

[*Exit.*

Lady A. Good Heavens! What noise is that?

Maid. Lord 'a mercy! The battle is coming?

Lady A. Hush! (*To a sentinel who goes whistling by.*) Sirrah, what noise is that?

Sentinel. It's these Indians, my lady; they have found the son of some chief of theirs murdered in these woods, and they are bringing him to the camp now. That's the mourning they make.

Lady A. The Lord protect us!

(They enter the house.)

DIALOGUE V.

SCENE. *The interior of a tent. Maitland, in travelling equipments, pacing the floor.*

Maitland. William! Ho there!

Servant. (*Looking in.*) Your honor?

Mait. Is not that horse ready yet?

Ser't. Presently, your honor.

[*Exit.*

Mait. So the fellow has been here, it seems, and returned again to Fort Edward without seeing me. Of course, my lady deigns no answer.—An answer! Well, I thought I expected none. Ten minutes ago I should have sworn I expected none. Why, by this time that letter of mine has gone the rounds of the garrison, no doubt. William!

(The servant enters.)

Bring that horse round, you rascal,—must I be under your orders too, forsooth?

Ser't. Certainly, your honor,—but if he could but just, —I am a-going, Sir,—but if he could but just take a mouthful or two more. There's never a baiting-place till—

Mait. Do you hear?

(The Servant retreats hastily.)

Mait. The curse of having lived in these wilds cleaves to me in all things. Here are Andre and Mortimer, and a hundred more, and none but I for this midnight service.

Ser't. (*Re-entering.*) The horse is waiting, Sir,—but here's two of these painted creturs hanging about the door, waiting to see you. (*Handing him a packet.*) There's no use in swearing at them, Sir, they don't understand it.

Mait. (*Breaking the seals hastily, he discovers the miniature.*) Back again! Well, we'll try drowning next,—nay, this is as I sent it! That rascal dropped it in the woods perhaps! Softly,—what have we here!

(*He discovers, and reads the letter.*)

Who brought this?

Ser't. The Indian that was here yesterday.

Mait. Alaska! Here's blood on the envelope, on the letter too, and here—This packet has been soaked in blood. (*Re-reading the letter.*)

"To-morrow"—"twelve o'clock" to-morrow—Look if the light be burning in the Lady Ackland's window,—she was up as I passed. "Twelve o'clock"—There are more horses on this route than these cunning settlers choose to reckon. Why, there are ten hours yet—I shall be back ere then. Helen—do I dream?—This is love!—How I have wronged her.—This *is* love!

Ser't. (*At the door.*) The horse is waiting, Sir,—and this Indian here wont stir till he sees you.

Mait. Alaska—I must think of it,—*risk?*—I would pledge my life on his truth. He has seen her too,—I remember now, he saw her—with me at the lake. Let him come in.—No, stop, I will speak with him as I go.

[*Exeunt.*

DIALOGUE VI.

SCENE. *Lady Ackland's door.*

Lady Ackland. Married!—His wife?—Well, I think I'll not try to sleep again. There goes Orion with his starry girdle.—Married—is he?

Maid. Was not that Captain Maitland that was talking here just now, Lady Harriet?

Lady A. Go to bed, Margaret,—go to bed,—but look you though. To-morrow with the dawn that furnishing gear we left in the tent must be unpacked, and this empty room—whose wife, think you, is my guest tomorrow, Margaret?

Maid. Bless me! If I were to guess till daylight, my lady—

Lady A. This young Maitland, you think so handsome, Margaret—

Maid. I?—la, it was not I, my lady, I am sure.

Lady A.—He will bring us his wife home here tomorrow, a young and beautiful wife.

Maid. Wife?—

Lady A. Poor child,—we must give her a gentle welcome. Do you remember those flowers we saw in the glen as we passed?—I will send for them in the morning, and we will fill the vacant hearth with these blossoming boughs.—

Maid. But, here—in these woods, a wife!—where on earth will he bring her from, my lady?

Lady A. Ay, we shall see, to-morrow we shall see,—go dream the rest.

[*Exit the maid.*

Lady A. Who would have thought it?—so cold and proud he seemed, so scornful of our sex.—And yet I knew something there lay beneath it all.—Even in that wild, gay mood, when the light of mirth filled and o'er-flowed those splendid eyes,—deeper still, I saw always the calm sorrow-beam shining within.

That picture he showed me—how pretty it was!—The face haunts me with its look of beseeching loveliness.—Was there anything so sorrowful about it though?—Nay, the look was a smile, and yet a strange mourn-fulness clings to my thought of it now. Well, if the painter hath not dissembled in it—the *painter*?—no. The spirit of those eyes was of no painter's making. From the *Eidos* of the Heavenly Mind sprung that.

I shall see her to-morrow.—Nay, I must meet her in the outskirts of the camp,—so went my promise,—if Maitland be not here ere then.

[*Exit.*

THOUGHTS.

SCENE. *The Hill. The Student's Night-watch.*

How beautiful the night, through all these hours
Of nothingness, with ceaseless music wakes
Among the hills, trying the melodies
Of myriad chords on the lone, darkened air,
With lavish power, self-gladdened, caring nought
That there is none to hear. How beautiful!
That men should live upon a world like this,
Uncovered all, left open every night
To the broad universe, with vision free
To roam the long bright galleries of creation,
Yet, to their strange destiny ne'er wake.
Yon mighty hunter in his silver vest,
That o'er those azure fields walks nightly now,
In his bright girdle wears the self-same gems
That on the watchers of old Babylon
Shone once, and to the soldier on her walls
Marked the swift hour, as they do now to me.

Prose is the dream, and poetry the truth.
That which we call reality, is but
Reality's worn surface, that one thought
Into the bright and boundless all might pierce,
There's not a fragment of this weary real
That hath not in its lines a story hid
Stranger than aught wild chivalry could tell.
There's not a scene of this dim, daily life,
But, in the splendor of one truthful thought
As from creation's palette freshly wet,
Might make young romance's loveliest picture dim,
And e'en the wonder-land of ancient song,—
Old Fable's fairest dream, a nursery rhyme.
How calm the night moves on, and yet
In the dark morrow, that behind those hills
Lies sleeping now, who knows what waits?—'Tis well.
He that made this life, I'll trust with another.
To be,—there was the risk. We might have waked
Amid a wrathful scene, but this,—with all
Its lovely ordinances of calm days,
The golden morns, the rosy evenings,

Its sweet sabbath hours and holy homes,—
If the same hidden hand from whence these sprung,
That dark gate opens, what need we fear there?—
Here's wrath, but none that hath not its sure pathway
Upward leading,—there are tears, but 'tis
A school-time weariness; and many a breeze
And lovely warble from our native hills,
Through the dim casement comes, over the worn
And tear-wet page, unto the listening ear
Of our home sighing—to the *listening* ear.
Ah, what know we of life?—of that strange life
That this, in many a folded rudiment,
With nature's low, unlying voice, doth point to.
Is it not very like what the poor grub
Knows of the butterfly's gay being?—
With its colors strange, fragrance, and song,
And robes of floating gold with gorgeous dyes,
And loveliest motion o'er wide, blooming worlds.
That dark dream had ne'er imaged!—
         Ay, sing on,
Sing on, thou bright one, with the news of life,
The everlasting, winging o'er our vale.
Oh warble on, thy high, strange song.
What sayest thou?—a land o'er these dark cliffs,
A land all glory, where the day ne'er setteth—
Where bright creatures, mid the deathless shades,
Go singing, shouting evermore? And yet
'Twere vain. That wild tale hath no meaning here,
Thou warbler from afar. Like music
Of a foreign tongue, on our dull sense,
The rich thought wastes.—We have been nursed in tears,
Thro' all we've known of life, we have known grief,
And is there none in life's deep essence mixed?
Is sorrow but the young soul's garment then?—
A baby mantle, doffed forever here,
Within these lowly walls.
        And we were born
Amid a glad creation!—-then why hear we ne'er
The silver shout, filling the unmeasured heaven?—
Why catch we e'er the rich plume's rustle soft,
Or sweep of passing lyre! Our tearful home
Hung 'mid a gay, rejoicing universe,
And ne'er a glimpse adown its golden paths?—
Oh are there eyes, soft eyes upon us,
In the dark and in the day, shining unseen,
And everlasting smiles, brightening unfelt
On all our tears: News sweet and strange ye bring.
Hither we came from our Creator's hands,

Bright earnest ones, looking for joy, and lo,
A stranger met us at the gate of life,
A stranger dark, and wrapped us in her robe,
And bore us on through a dim vale.—Ah, not
The world we looked for,—for an image in.
Our souls was born, of a high home, that yet
We have not seen. And were our childhood's yearnings,
Its strange hopes, no dreams then,—dim revealings
Of a land that yet we travel to?—
But thou, oh foster-mother, mournful nurse,
So long upon thy sable vest we're leaned,
Thou art grown dear to us, and when at last
At yonder blue and burning gate
Thou yieldest up thy trust, and joy at last
In her own wild embrace enfolds us once, e'en
From the jewelled bosom of that dazzling one,
From the young roses of that smiling face,
Shall we not turn to thee, for one last glimpse
Of that wan cheek, and solemn eye of love,
And watch thy stately step, far down
This dim world's fading paths? Take us, kind sorrow!
We will lean our young head meekly on thee;
Good and holy is thy ministry,
Oh handmaid of the Halls thou ne'er mayst tread.
And let the darkness gather round that world,
Not for the vision of thy glittering walls
We ask, nor glimpse of brilliant troops that roam
Thine ancient streets, thou sunless city,—
Wrap thy strange pavillions still in clouds,
Let the shades slumber round thy many homes,
By faith, and not by sight, through lowly paths
Of goodness, sorrow-led, to thee we come.

PART FOURTH.

FULFILMENT.

DIALOGUE I.

SCENE. *The ground before the fort. Baggage wagons. Cannon dismounted. Confused sounds within. A soldier is seen leaning on his rifle.*

(*Another soldier enters.*)

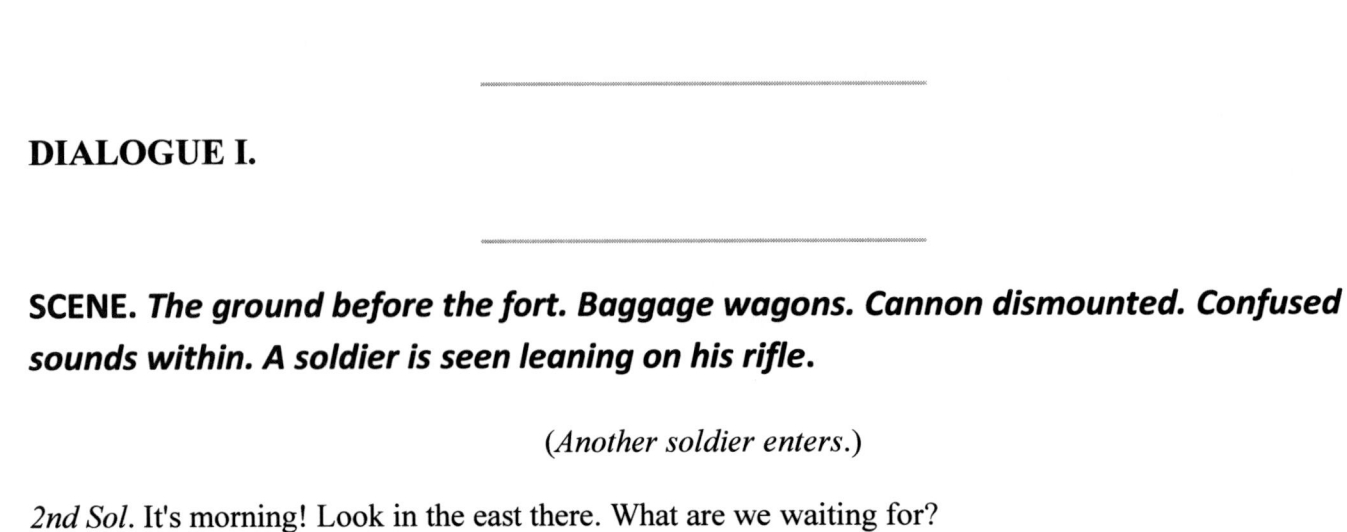

2nd Sol. It's morning! Look in the east there. What are we waiting for?

1st Sol. Eh! The devil knows best, I reckon, Sir.

2nd Sol. Hillo, John! What's the matter there? Here's day-break upon us! What are we waiting for?

(*Another soldier enters.*)

3d Sol. To build a bridge—that is all.

2nd Sol. A bridge?

3d Sol. We shall be off by to-morrow night, no doubt of it,—if we don't chance to get cooked and eaten before that time,—some little risk of that.

2nd Sol. But what's the matter below there, I say? The bridge? what ails it?

3d Sol. Just as that last wagon was going over, down comes the bridge, Sirs, or a good piece of it at least.—What else could it do?—timbers half sawn away!

2nd Sol. Some of that young jackanape's work! *Aid-de-camp!* I'd *aid* him. He must be ordering and fidgetting, and fuming.—Could not wait till we were over.

1st Sol. All of a piece, boys!

3d Sol. Humph. I wish it had been,—the bridge, I mean.

1st Sol. But, I say, don't you see how every thing, little and great, goes one way, and that, against us? Chance has no currents like this! It's a bad side that Providence frowns on. I think when Heaven deserts a cause, it's time for us poor mortals to begin to think about it.

3d Sol. Now, if you are going to do so mean a thing as that, don't talk about Heaven—prythee don't.

[*They pass on.*

(*Two other soldiers enter.*)

4th Sol. (*singing.*)
>Yankee doodle is the tune
> Americans delight in,
> 'Twill do to whistle, sing, or play,
>   And just the thing for fighting.
> Yankee doodle, boys, huzza—

(*Breaking off abruptly.*) I do not like the looks of it, Will.

5th Sol. Of what?

4th Sol. Of the morning that begins to glimmer in the east there.

5th Sol. No? Why, I was thinking just now I never saw a handsomer summer's dawning. That first faint light on the woods and meadows, there is nothing I like better. See, it has reached the river now.

4th Sol. But the mornings we saw two years ago looked on us with another sort of eye than this,—it is not the glimmer of the long, pleasant harvest day that we see there.

5th Sol. We have looked on mornings that promised better, I'll own. I would rather be letting down the bars in the old meadow just now, or hawing with my team down the brake; with the children by my side to pick the ripe blackberries for our morning meal, than standing here in these rags with a gun on my shoulder. Let well alone.—We could not though.

4th Sol. (*Handing him a glass.*) See, they are beginning to form again. It looks for all the world like a funeral train.

5th Sol. What was the Stamp Act to us, or all the acts beyond the sea that ever were acted, so long as they left us our golden fields, our Sabbath days, the quiet of the summer evening door, and the merry winter hearth. *The Stamp Act?* It would have been cheaper for us to have written our bills on gold-leaf, and for tea, to have drunk melted jewels, like the queen I read of once; cheaper and better, a thousand times, than the bloody cost we are paying now.

4th Sol. It was not the money, Will,—it was not the money, you know. The wrong it was. We could not be trampled on in that way,—it was not in us—we could not.

5th Sol. Ay, ay. A fine thing to get mad about was that when we sat in the door of a moonlight evening and the day's toils were done. It was easy talking then. *Trampled on!* I will tell you when I was nearest being trampled on, Andros,—when I lay on the ground below there last winter,—on the frozen ground, with the blood running out of my side like a river, and a great high-heeled German walking over my shoulder as if I had been a hickory log. I can tell you, Sir, that other was a moon-shiny sort of a trampling to that. I shall bear to be trampled on in figures the better for it, as long as I live. Between ourselves now—

4th Sol. There's no one here.

5th Sol. There are voices around that corner, though. Come this way.

[*They pass on.*

(*Another group of Soldiers.*)

1st Sol. Then if nothing else happens, we are off now. Hillo, Martin! Here we go again—skulking away. Hey? What do you say now? Hey, Mr. Martin, what do you say now?

2nd Sol. (*Advancing.*) What I said before.

1st Sol. But where is all this to end, Sir? Tell us that—tell us that.

3d Sol. Yes, yes,—tell us that. If you don't see Burgoyne safe in Albany by Friday night, never trust me, Sirs.

1st Sol. A bad business we've made of it.

4th Sol. Suppose he gets to Albany;—do you think that would finish the war?

3d Sol. Well, indeed, I thought that was settled on all hands, Sir. I believe the General himself makes no secret of that.

4th Sol. And what becomes of us all then? We shall go back to the old times again, I suppose;—weren't so very bad though, Sam, were they?

1st Sol. We have seen worse, I'll own.

3d Sol. And what becomes of our young nation here, with its congress and its army, and all these presidents, and generals, and colonels, and aide-de-camps?—wont it look like a great baby-house when the hubbub is over, and the colonies settle quietly down again?

2nd Sol. Faith, you take it very coolly. Before that can happen, do you know what must happen to you?

1st Sol. Nothing worse than this, I reckon.

2nd Sol. (*makes a gesture to denote hanging.*)

4th Sol. What would they hang us though? Do you think they would really hang us, John?

2nd Sol. Wait and see.

1st Sol. Nonsense! nonsense! A few of the ringleaders, Schuyler, and Hancock, and Washington, and a few such, they will hang of course,—but for the rest,—we shall have to take the oath anew, and swallow a few duties with our sugar and tea, and—

2nd Sol. You talk as if the matter were all settled already.

1st Sol. There is no more doubt of it, than that you and I stand here this moment. Why, they are flocking to Skeensborough from all quarters now, and this poor fragment,—this miserable skeleton of an army, which is the only earthly obstacle between Burgoyne and Albany, why, even this is crumbling to pieces as fast as one can reckon. Two hundred less than we were yesterday at this hour, and to-morrow—how many are off to-morrow? Ay, and what are we doing the while? Bowing and retreating, cap in hand, from post to post, from Crown Point to Ticonderoga, from Ticonderoga to Fort Edward, from Fort Edward onward; just showing them down, as it were, into the heart of the land. Let them get to Albany—Ah, let them once get to Albany, they'll need no more of our help then, they'll take care of themselves then and us too.

2nd Sol. They'll never get to Albany.

1st Sol. Hey?

2nd Sol. They'll never get to Albany.

1st Sol. What's to hinder them?

2nd Sol. We,—yes we,—and such as we, craven-hearted as we are. They'll never get to Albany until we take them there captives.

3d Sol. Then they'll wait till next week, I reckon.

1st Sol. Ha ha ha! Ha ha ha! How many prisoners shall we have a-piece, John? How many regiments, I mean? They'll open the windows when we get there, won't they? I hope the sun will shine that day. How grandly we shall march down the old hill there, with our train behind us. I shall have to borrow a coat of one of them though, they might be ashamed of their captor else.

3d Sol. When is this great battle to be, John? This don't look much like it.

4th Sol. I think myself, if the General would only give us a chance to fight—

2nd Sol. A chance to throw your life away,—he will never give you. A chance to fight, you will have ere long,—doubt it not. Our General might clear his blackened fame, by opposing this force to that,—this day he might;—he will not do it. The time has not yet come. But he will spare no pains to strengthen the army, and prepare it for victory, and the glory he will leave to his rival. Recruits will be pouring in ere long. General Burgoyne's proclamation has weakened us,—General Schuyler will issue one himself to-day.

1st Sol. Will he? will he? What will he proclaim?—As to the recruits he gets, I'll eat them all, skin and bone. What will he proclaim? You see what Burgoyne offers us. On the one hand, money and clothing, and protection for ourselves and our families; and on the other, the cord, and the tomahawk, and the scalping-knife. Now, what will General Schuyler set down over against these two columns?—What will he offer us?—To lend us a gun, maybe,—leave to follow him from one post to another, barefooted and starving, and for our pains to be cursed and reviled for cowards from one end of the land to the other. And what will he threaten? Ha, we were cowards indeed, if we feared what he could threaten. What thing in human nature will he speak to?—say.

2nd Sol. I will tell you. To that spirit in human nature which resists the wrong, the fiendish wrong threatened there. Ay, in the basest nature that power sleeps, and out of the bosom of Omnipotence there is nothing stronger. It has wakened here once, and this war is its fruit. It slumbers now. Let Burgoyne look to it that he rouse it not himself for us. Let him look to it. For every outrage of those fiendish legions, thank God.—It lays a finger on the spring of our only strength. *What* will he offer us? I will tell you.—A chance to live, or to die,—*men*,—ay, to leave a sample of manhood on the earth, that shall wring tears from the selfish of unborn ages, as they feel for once the depths of the slumbering and godlike nature within them. And Burgoyne,—oh! a coat and a pair of shoes, he offers, and—how many pounds?—Are you men?

4th Sol. What do you say, Sam?—Talks like a minister, don't he?

1st Sol. Come, come,—there's the drum, boys. You don't bamboozle me again! I've heard all that before.

3d Sol. Nor me.—I don't intend to have my wife and children tomahawked,—don't think I can stand that, refugee or not.

2nd Sol. Here they come.

(*Other Soldiers enter.*)

5th Sol. All's ready, all's ready.

6th Sol. (*singing.*)
"*Come blow the shrill bugle, the war dogs are howling,*"—

[Exeunt.

DIALOGUE II.

SCENE. *Before the door of the Parsonage. Trunks, boxes, and various articles of furniture, scattered about the yard. Two men coming down the path.*

(*George Grey enters.*)

George. Those trunks in the forward team. Make haste. We've no time to lose. This box in the wagon where the children are.—Carefully—carefully, though.

(*A Soldier enters.*)

Sol. Hurra, hurra, the house there! Are you ready? Ten minutes more.

George. Get out. What do you stand yelling there for? We know all about it.

Sol. But your brother, the Captain, says, I must hurry you, or you'll be left behind.

George. Tell my brother, the Captain, I'll see to that. We want no more hurrying. We have had enough of that already, and much good it has done us too. Stop, stop,—not that. We must leave those for the Indians to take their tea in.

Workman. But the lady said—

George. Never mind the lady. Well, Annie, are you ready? Don't stand there crying; there's no use. We may come back here again yet, you know. Many a pleasant sunrise we may see from these windows yet. Heaven defend us, here is this aunt of ours.—What on earth are they bringing now?

(*A Lady in the door with a couple of portraits, followed by others bringing baskets and boxes, etc.*)

Lady. That will do, set them down; now, the Colonel and his lady, on the back room wall, just over against the beaufet. Stop a moment. I'll go with you myself.

Betty. (In, the door.) Lord 'a mercy! Here it is broad day-light. What are we waiting for? I am all ready. Why don't we go?

George. I tell you, Aunt Rachael, the thing is impossible. This trumpery can't go, and there's the end of it. St. George and the Dragon—

Miss Rachael. Never mind this young malapert—do as I bid you.

Betty. Lord 'a mercy, we shall all be murdered and scalped, every soul of us. Bless you—there it is in the garret now!—just hold this umberell a minute, Mr. George,—think of those murderous Indians wearing my straw bonnet. Lord bless you! What are you doing? a heaving my umberell over the fence, in that fashion!

George. These women will drive me mad I believe. Let that box alone, you rascal. Lay a finger on that trumpery there I say, and you'll find whose orders you are under; as for the Colonel and his lady, they'll get a little drink out of the first puddle we come to, I reckon.

[*Goes out.*

Miss R. (*Coming from the house.*) That will do. That is all,—in the green wagon, John—

Ser't. But the children—

Miss R. Don't stand there, prating to me at a time like this. Make haste, make haste!

How perfectly calm I am! I would never have believed it;—just tie this string for me, child, my hands twitch so strangely,—they say the British are just down in the lane here, with five thousand Indians, Annie.

Annie. It is no such thing. Aunt Rachael. The British are quietly encamped on the other side of the river; three miles off at least.

Miss R. I thought as much. A pretty hour for us to be turned out of house and home to be sure. Not a wink have I slept this blessed night. Hark! What o'clock is that? George, George! where is that boy? Just run and tell your mother, Annie, just tell her, my dear, will you, that we shall all be murdered. Maybe she will make haste a little. Well, are they in?

Ser't. The pictures? They are in,—yes'm. But Miss Kitty's a crying, and says as how she won't go, and there's the other one too; because, Ma'am, their toes—you see there's the trunk in front gives 'em a leetle slope inward, and then that chest under the seat—If you would just step down and see yourself, Ma'am.

Miss R. I desire to be patient.

[*They go out.*

(*Annie sits on the bench of the little Porch, weeping. Mrs. Gray enters from within.*)

Annie. Shall I never walk down that shady path again? Shall I enter those dear rooms no more? There are voices there they cannot hear. From the life of buried years, ten thousand scenes, all vacancy toother eyes, enrich those walls for us; the furniture that money cannot buy, that only the joy and grief of years can purchase. They will spoil our pleasant home,—will they not, mother?

Mrs. G. Pleasant, ay, pleasant indeed, has it been to us. God's will be done. Do not weep, Annie. We have counted the cost;—many a safe and happy home there will be in the days to come, whose light shall spring from this forgotten sorrow. God's will be done.

Annie. Mother, they are all ready now; is Helen in her room still?

Mrs. G. Go call her, Annie. Hours ago it was I sent her there. I thought she might get some little sleep ere the summons came. Call her, my child. How deadly pale she was!

[*Annie goes in.*

DIALOGUE III.

SCENE. *A Chamber partly darkened, the morning air steals faintly through the half-open shutters. Helen before the mirror, leaning upon the toilette, her face buried in her hands, her long hair unbound, and flowing on her shoulders.*

(*Annie enters.*)

Annie. Helen! Why, Helen, are you asleep there? Come, we are going now. After keeping us on tiptoe for hours, the summons has come at last. Indeed, there is hardly time for you to dress. Shall I help you?

Helen. (*Rising slowly.*) God help me. Bid my mother come here, Annie.

Annie. What ails you, Helen?—there is no time,—you do not understand me,—there is not one moment to be lost. Let me wind up this hair for you.

Helen. Let go!—Oh God—

Annie. Helen Grey!

Helen. It was a dream,—it was but a foolish dream. It must not be thought of now,—it will never do. Bid my mother come here, I am ready now.

Annie. Ready, Helen!—ready?—in that dressing-gown, and your hair—see here,—are you ready, Helen?

Helen. Yes,—bid her come.

Annie. Heaven only knows what you mean with this wild talk of yours, but if you are not mad indeed, I intreat you, sister, waste no more of this precious time.

Helen. No, no,—we must not indeed. It was wrong, but I could not—go,—make haste, bid her come.

Annie. She is crazed, certainly!

[*Goes out.*

(*Helen stands with her arms folded, and her eye fixed on the door.*)

(*Mrs. Grey enters.*)

Mrs. G. My child! Helen, Helen! Why do you stand there thus?

Helen. Mother—

Mrs. G. Nay, do not stay to speak. There—throw this mantle around you. Where is your hat?—not here!—Bridal gear!

The Bride of Fort Edward: Founded on an Incident of the Revolution

(*George enters.*)

George. On my word! Well, well, stand there a little longer, to dress those pretty curls of yours, and — humph—there's a style in vogue in yonder camp for rebels just now; we'll all stand a chance to try, I think.

Helen. George!—George Grey!—Be still,—be still.— We must not think of that. It was a dream.

George. Is my sister mad?

Helen. Mother—

Mrs. G. Speak, my child.

Helen. Mother—my blessed mother,—(*aside.*) 'Tis but a brief word,—it will be over soon.

Mrs. G. Speak, Helen.

Helen. I cannot go with you, mother.

Mrs. G. Helen?

George. Not go with us?

Mrs. G. Helen, do you know what you are saying?

George. You are in jest, Helen; or else you are mad,—before another sunset the British army will be encamping here.

Helen. Hear me, mother. A message from the British camp came to me last night,—

Mrs. G. The British camp?—Ha!—ha! Everard Maitland! God forgive him.

Helen. Do not speak thus. It was but a few cold and careless lines he sent me,—my purpose is my own.

Mrs. G. And—what, and he does not know?—Helen Grey, this passes patience.

Helen. He does, Here is the answer that has just now come; for I have promised to meet him to-day at the hut of the missionary in yonder woods.—I can hardly spell these hasty words; but this I know, he will surely come for me,—though he bids me wait until I hear his signal,—so I cannot go with you, mother.

Mrs. G. Where will you go, Helen?

Helen. Everard is in yonder camp;—where should the wife's home be?

Mrs. G. The wife's?

Helen. These two years I have been his bride;—his wedded wife I shall be to-day. Yonder dawns my bridal day.

George. What does she say? What does Helen say? I do not understand one word of it.

Mrs. G. She says she will go to the British camp. Desertions thicken upon us. Hark!—they are calling us.

George. To the British camp?

Mrs. G. Go down, George, go down. Your sister talks wildly and foolishly, what you should not have heard, what she will be sorry for anon; go down, and tell them they must wait for us a little,—we will be there presently.

George. Hark! (*going to the door.*)—another message. Do you hear?—Helen may be ready yet, if she will.

Mrs. G. Blessed delay! Go down, George; say nothing of this. There is time yet. Tell them we will be there presently.

(*George goes out.*)

Mrs. G. Did you think I should leave you here to accomplish this frantic scheme?—Did you dream of it, and you call me mother?—but what do you know of that name's meaning? Do not turn away from me thus, my child; do not stand with that fixed eye as though some phantom divinity were there. I shall not leave you here, Helen, never.

Come, come; sit down with me in this pleasant window, there is time yet,—let us look at this moonlight scheme of yours a little. Would you stay here in this deserted citadel, alone? My child, our army are already on their march. In an hour more you would be the only living thing in all this solitude. Would you stay here alone, to meet your lover too?—Bethink yourself, Helen.

Helen. This Canadian girl will stay with me, and—

Mrs. G. A girl!—Helen, yesterday an army's strength, the armies of the nation, the love of mother, and brothers, and sisters, all seemed nothing for protection to your timid and foreboding thought; and now, when the enemy are all around us,—do you talk of a single girl? Why, the spirit of some strange destiny is struggling with your nature, and speaks within you, but we will not yield to it.

Helen. You have spoken truly, mother. There is one tie in these hearts of ours, whose strength makes destiny, and where that leads, there lie those iron ways that are of old from everlasting. This is Heaven's decree, not mine.

Mrs. G. Do not charge the madness of this frantic scheme on Heaven, my child.

Helen. Everard!—no, no, I cannot show to another the lightning flash, that with that name reveals my destiny,—yet the falling stone might as soon—question of its way. Renounce him?—you know not what you ask! all there is of life within me laughs at the wild impossibility.

Mother, hear me. There is no danger in my staying here,—none real. The guard still keep their station on yonder hill, and the fort itself will not be wholly abandoned to-day. Everard will come for me at noon.—It is impossible that the enemy should be here ere then; nay, the news of this unlooked-for movement will scarce have reached their camp.—*Real* danger there is none, and—Do not urge me. I know what you would say; the bitter cost I have counted all, already, all—*all*. That Maitland is in yonder camp, that—is it not a strange blessedness which can sweeten anguish such as this?—that he loves me still, that he will come here to-day to make me his forever,—this is all that I can say, my mother.

Mrs. G. Will you go over to the British side, Helen? Will you go over to the side of wrong and oppression? Would you link yourself with our cruel and pursuing enemy? Oh no, no no,—that could not be—never, Amid the world of fearful thoughts that name brings, how could we place your image? Oh God, I did not count on this. I knew that this war was to bring us toil, and want, and fear, and haply bloody death; and I could have borne it unmurmuringly; but—God forgive me,—that the child I nursed in these arms should forsake me, and join with our deadly foes against us—I did not count on this.

Helen. Yes—that's the look,—the very look—all night I saw it;—it does not move me now, as it did then. It is shadows of these things that are so fearful, for with the real comes the unreckoned power of suffering. Mother, this dark coil hath Heaven wound, not we. The tie which makes his path the way of God to me, was linked ere this war was,—and war cannot undo it now. It is a bitter fate, I know,—a bitter and a fearful one.

Mrs. G. Ay, ay,—thank God! You had forgotten, Helen, that in that army's pay, nay, all around us even now are hordes and legions.

Helen. I know it,—I know it all. I do indeed.

Mrs. G. Helen, will you place yourself defenceless amidst that savage race, whose very name from your childhood upwards, has filled you with such strange fear? Yesterday I chid you for those fancies,—I was wrong,—they were warnings, heaven-sent, to save you from this doom. What was that dream you talked of then?

Helen. Dreams are nothing. Will you unsay a life's lessons now when most I need them?

Mrs. G. Yesterday, all day, a shadow as of coming evil lay upon me, but now I remember the forgotten vision whence it fell. Yesternight I had a dream, Helen, such as yours might be; for in my broken and fevered slumbers, wherever I turned, one vision awaited me. There was a savage arm, and over it fell a shower of golden hair, and ever and anon, in the shadowy light of my dream, a knife glittered and waved before me. We were safe, but over one,—some young and innocent and tender one it was—there hung a hopeless and inexorable fate. Once methought it seemed the young English girl that was wedded here last winter, and once she turned her eye upon me—Ha!—I had forgotten that glance of agony—surely, Helen, it was *yours*.

Mrs. G. Helen! my child—(*Aside.*) There it is, that same curdling glance,—'twas but a dream, Helen. Why do you stand there so white and motionless—why do you look on me with that fixed and darkening eye?—'twas but a dream!

Helen. And where were you?—tell me truly. Was it not by a gurgling fountain among the pine trees there? and was it not noon-day in your dream, a hot, bright, sultry noon, and a few clouds swelling in the western sky, and nothing but the trilling locusts astir?

Mrs. G. How wildly you talk; how should I remember any thing like this?

Helen. I will not yield to it; tempt me not. 'Tis folly all, I know it is. Danger there is none. Long ere yonder hill is abandoned, Everard will be here; and who knows that I am left here alone, and who would come here to seek me out but he? Oh no, I cannot break this solemn faith for a dream. What would he give to know I held my promise and his love lighter than a dream? I must *stay* here, mother.

Mrs. G. No, my child. Hear me. If this must be indeed, if all my holy right in you is nothing, if you will indeed go over to our cruel enemy, and rejoice in our sorrows and triumph in our overthrow—

Helen. Hear her—

Mrs. G. Be it so, Helen,—be it so; but for all that, do not stay here to-day. Bear but a little longer with our wearisome tenderness, and wait for some safer chance of forsaking us. Come.

Helen. If I could—Ah, if I could—

Mrs. G. You can—you will. Here, let me help you, we shall be ready yet. No one knows of this wild scheme but your brother and myself, no one else shall ever know it. Come.

Helen. If I could. 'Tis true, I did not know when I sent him this promise you would leave me alone ere the hour should come. Perhaps—no, it would never do. When he comes and finds that, after all, I have deserted him, once with a word I angered him, and for years it was the last between us;—and what safer chance will there be in these fearful times of meeting him? No, no. If we do not meet now, we are parted for ever;—if I do not keep my promise now, I shall see him no more.

Mrs. G. See him no more then. What is he to us—this stranger, this haughty, all-requiring one? Think of the blessed days ere he had crossed our threshold. You have counted all, Helen? The anguish that will bring tears into your proud brother's eyes, your sister's comfortless sorrow?—did you think of her lonely and saddened youth? You counted the wild suffering of this bitter moment,—did you think of the weary years, the long sleepless nights of grief, the days of tears; did you count the anguish of a mother's broken heart, Helen? God only can count that.

You did not—there come the blessed tears at last. Here's my own gentle daughter, once again. Come, Helen, see, they are waiting for us. There stands the old chaise under the locust tree. You and I will ride together. Come, 'tis but a few steps down that shady path, and we are safe—a few steps and quickly trod. Hark! the respite is past even now. Do you stand there marble still? Helen, if you stay here, we shall see you no more. This lover of yours hates us all. He will take you to England when the war is over if you outlive its bloody hazards, and we are parted for ever. I shall see you no more, Helen, my child; my child, I shall see you no more. (*She sinks upon the chair, and weeps aloud.*)

Helen. Has it come to this? Will you break my heart? If it were continents and oceans that you bade me cross, but those few steps—Ah, they would sever me from him for ever, and I cannot, I cannot, I can *not* take them,—there is no motion so impossible. Yes, they are calling us. Do not stay.

(*Annie enters.*)

Annie. Mother, will you tell me what this means?

Mrs. G. Yes, come in. We will waste no more time about it. She will stay here to meet her lover, she will forsake us for a traitor. We have nursed an enemy among us. The babe I cherished in this bosom, whose sleeping face I watched with a young mother's love, hath become my enemy. Oh my God—is it from thee?

Annie. Helen! my sister! Helen!

Mrs. G. Ay, look at her. Would you think that the spirit which heaves in that light frame, and glances in those soft eyes, held such cruel power? Yesterday I would have counted it a breath in the way of my lightest purpose, and now—come away, Annie—it is vain, you cannot move her.

(*George enters.*)

George. Mother, if Helen will not go now, we must leave her to her fate or share it with her. Every wagon is on the road but ours. A little more, and we shall be too late for the protection of the army. Shall I stay with her?

Mrs. G. No, never. That were a sure and idle waste of life. Helen, perhaps, may be safe with them. Oh. yes, the refugees are safe, else desertion would grow out of fashion soon.

Annie. Refugees! Refugee! Helen!

Mrs. G. It sounds strange for one of us I know. You will grow used to it soon. Helen belongs to the British side, she will go over to them to-day, but she must go alone, for none of us would be safe in British hands, at least I trust so—this morning's experience might make me doubtful, but I trust we are all true here yet beside.

Annie. Have I heard aright, Helen?—or is this all some fearful dream? You and I, who have lived together all the years of our lives, to be parted this moment, and for ever,—no, no!

(*A young American Officer enters hastily.*)

Capt. Grey. Softly, softly! What is this? Are you in this conspiracy to disgrace me, mother? Oh, very well; if you have all decided to stay here, I'll take my leave.

Annie. Oh, Henry, stay. You can persuade her it may be.

Capt. G. Persuade! What's all this! A goodly time for rhetoric forsooth! Who's this that's risking all our lives, waiting to be persuaded now?

Mrs. G. That Tory, Henry! We should have thought of this. Ah, if we had gone yesterday,—that haughty Maitland,—she will stay here to meet him! She will marry him, my son.

Capt. G. Maitland!—and stay here!

Helen. Dear Henry, let us part in kindness. Do not look on me with that angry eye. It was I that played with you in the woods and meadows, it was I that roamed with you in those autumn twilights,—you loved me then, and we are parting for ever it may be..

Capt. G. (*To the children at the door.*) Get you down, young ones, get you down. Pray, mother, lead the way, will you?—break up this ring. Come, Helen, you and I will talk of this as we go on, only in passing give me leave to say, of all the mad pranks of your novel ladies, this caps the chief. You have outdone them, Helen; I'll give you credit for it, you have outdone them all.

Why you'll be chronicled,—there's nothing on record like it, that ever I heard of; I am well-read in romances too. We'll have a new love-ballad made and set to tune, under the head of "Love and Murder," it will come though, if you don't make haste a little. Come, come.

Helen. Henry!

Capt. G. Are you in earnest, Helen? Did you suppose that we were mad enough to leave you here? You'll not go with us? But you will, by Heaven!

Helen. Henry! Mother!—Nay, Henry, this is vain. I shall stay here, I shall—I shall stay here,—so help me Heaven.

Capt. G. Helen Grey! Is that young lioness there my sometime sister?—my delicate sister?—with her foot planted like iron, and the strength of twenty men nerving her arm?

Helen. Let go.—I shall stay here.

Capt. G. Well, have your way, young lady, have your way; but—Mother, if you choose to leave that mad girl here, you can,—but as for this same Everard Maitland, look you, my lady, if I don't stab him to his heart's core, never trust me.

(*He goes out—Mrs. Grey follows him to the door.*)

Mrs. G. Stay, Henry,—stay. What shall we do?

Capt. G. Do!—Indeed, a straight waistcoat is the only remedy I know of, Madam, for such freaks as these. If you say so, she shall go with us yet.

Mrs. G. Hear me. This is no time for passion now Hear me, Henry. This Maitland, *Tory* as he is, is her betrothed husband, and she has chosen her fate with him; we cannot keep her with us; nay, with what we have now seen, it would be vain to think of it, to wish it even. She must go to him,—it but remains to see that she meets him safely. Noon is the hour appointed for his coming. Could we not stay till then?

Capt. G. Impossible. Noon?—well.—Oh, if its all fixed upon;—if you have settled it between yourselves that Helen is to abandon us and our protection, for Everard Maitland's and the British, the sooner done, the better. She's quite right,—she's like to find no safer chance for it than this. Noon,—there is a picket left on yonder hill till after that time, certainly, and a hundred men or so in the fort. I might give Van Vechten a hint of it—nay, I can return myself this afternoon, and if she is not gone then, I will take it upon me she is not left a second time. Of course Maitland would be likely to care for her safety. At all events there's nothing else for us to do, at least there's but one alternative, and that I have named to you.

[*They go out together.*

Helen. (*She has stood silently watching them.*) He has gone, without one parting look—he has gone! So break the myriad-tied loves, it hath taken a life to weave. This is a weary world.

(*She turns to her sister, who leans weeping on the window-seat.*)

Come, Annie, you and I will part in kindness, will we not? No cruel words shall there be here. Pleasant hath your love been unto me, my precious sister. Farewell, Annie.

Annie. Shall I never hear your voice again, that hath been the music of my whole life? Is your face henceforth to be to me only a remembered thing? Helen, you must not stay here. The Indians,—it was no idle fear, the half of their bloody outrages you have not heard; they will murder you, yes, *you*. The innocence and loveliness that is holy to us, is nothing in their eyes, they would as soon sever that beautiful hair from your brow—

Helen. Hush, hush. There is no danger, Annie. The dark things of destiny are God's; the heart, the heart only, is ours.

(*Mrs. Grey re-enters.*)

Mrs. G. (*to Annie.*) Come, come, my child. This is foolish now. All is ready. Janette will stay with you, Helen.

(*Laughing voices are heard without, and the children's faces are seen peeping in the door.*)

Willy. Dear mother, are you not ready yet? We have been in the wagon and out a hundred times. Oh, Helen, make haste. The sun is above the trees, and the grass on the roadside is all full of diamonds. The last soldiers are winding down the hollow now. Is not Helen going, Mother?

Mrs. G. Your sister Helen is going from us forever. Come in and kiss her once, and then make haste—you must not all be lost.

(*They enter.*)

Willy. Ah, why don't you go with us, sister?—Such a beautiful ride we shall have. You never heard such a bird-singing in all your life.

Frank. We shall go by the Chesnut Hollow, George says we shall. Smell of these roses, Helen. Must she stay here? Hark, Willy, there's the drum. Good-bye, How sorry I am you will not go with us.

Willy. So am I. What makes you stand so still and look at us so? Why don't you kiss me? Good-bye, Helen.

Helen. (*Embracing them silently.*)

Annie. Will you leave her here alone, mother? Will you?

Mrs. G. No. There is a guard left on yonder hill, and the fort is not yet abandoned wholly. Besides, the army encamp at the creek, and Henry himself will return this afternoon. She will be gone ere then, though.

Helen. Those merry steps and voices, those little, soft clinging hands and rosy lips, have vanished forever. For all my love I shall be to them but as the faint trace of some faded dream. This is a weary world.

Come, George, farewell. How I have loved to look on that young brow. Be what my dreams have made you. Fare you well.

George. Farewell, Helen.

[*He goes out hastily.*

Helen. Will he forget me?

Mrs. G. And farewell, Helen. Fare ye well.

Helen. Will she leave me thus?

Mrs. G. Do not go to the hut—do not leave this door until you are sure of the signal you spoke of, Helen.

Helen. She will not look at me,—Mother!

Mrs. G. Farewell, Helen; may the hour never come when you need the love you have cast from you now so freely.

Helen. Will you leave me thus? Is not our life together ending here? In that great and solemn Hereafter our ways may meet again; but by the light of sun, or moon, or candle, or underneath these Heavens, no more. Oh! lovely, lovely have you been unto me, a spirit of holiness and beauty, building all my way.— Part we thus?

Mrs. G. Farewell, Helen.

Helen. Part we thus?

Mrs. G. Fare ye well, Helen Grey, my own sweet and precious child, my own lovely, lovely daughter, fare ye well, and the Lord be with you. The Lord keep you, for I can keep you now no more. The Lord watch over you, my helpless one, mine, mine, mine, all mine, though I leave you thus; my world of untold wealth, unto another. Nay, do not sorrow, my blessed child,—you will be happy yet. Fear nothing,—if this must be, I say, fear nothing. You think that you are doing right in forsaking us thus;—it may be that you are. If in the strength of a pure conscience you stay here to-day,—be not afraid. When you lay here of old, a lisping babe, I told you of One whose love was better than a mother's. Now farewell, and trust in Him. Farewell, mine eye shall see thee yet again. Farewell.

Helen. No, no; leave me not.

Mrs. G. Unclasp these hands, I cannot stay.

Helen. Never—never.

Mrs. G. Untwine this wild embrace, or, even now,—even now—

Helen. Farewell, mother. Annie Grey, farewell.

[*They go.*

Helen. This is a weary world. Take me home. To the land where there is no crying or bitterness, take me home.

(*The noise of retreating steps is heard, and the sound of the outer door closing heavily.*)

Helen. They are gone,—not to church,—not for the summer's ride. I shall see them no more.—In heaven it may be; but by the twilight hearth, or merry table, at morn, or noon, or evening, in mirth or earthly tenderness, no more.

Hark! There it is!—that voice,—I hear it now, I do. A dark eternity had rolled between us, and I hear it yet again. They are going now. Those rolling wheels, oh that that sound would last. There is no music half so sweet. Fainter—fainter—it is gone—no—that was but the hollow.—Hark—

Now they are gone, indeed. So breaks the sense's last link between me and that world.

PART FIFTH.

FULFILLMENT

DIALOGUE I.

SCENE. *The hill. A young Soldier enters*.

How gloriously, with what a lonely majesty the morning wastes in that silent valley there; with its moving shadows, and breeze and sunshine, and its thousand delicious sounds mocking those desolate homes—

(*He stops suddenly, and looks earnestly into the thicket.*)

This is strange, indeed. This feeling that I cannot analyze, still grows upon me. *Presentiment?* Some dark, swift-flying thought, leaves its trace, and the cause-seeking mind, in the range of its own vision finding none, looks to the shadowy future for it.

[*He passes on.*

(*Two Indian Chiefs, in their war-dress, emerge from the thicket, talking in suppressed tones.*)

1st Chief. Hoogh! Hoogh! Alaska fights to revenge his son,—we spill our blood to revenge his son, and he thinks to win gifts besides. Hugh! A brave chief he is!

2nd Chief. Your talk is not good, Manida. They are our enemies,—we shall conquer them, we shall see their chestnut locks waving aloft, we shall dance and shout all night around them, and the eyes of the maidens shall meet ours in the merry ring, sparkling with joy, as we shout "Victory! victory! our enemies are slain,—our foot is on their necks, we have slain our enemies!" What more, Manida? Is it not enough?

1st Chief. No. I went last night with Alaska to the camp above, to the tent of the young sachem of the lake, and he promised him presents, rich and many, for an errand that a boy might do. I asked Alaska to send me for him, and he would not.

2nd Chief. The young white sachem was Alaska's friend, many moons ago, when Alaska was wounded and sick.—He must revenge young Siganaw, but he must keep his faith to his white friend, too.

1st Chief. Ah, but I know where the horse is hidden and the paper. When the tomahawks flash here, and the war-cry is loudest, we will steal away. Come, and I will share the prize with you.

2nd Chief. No, I will tell my brother chief that Manida is a treacherous friend.

1st Chief. You cannot. It is too late. Hist! Quick, lower—lower—

[*They crouch among the trees.*

(*Another Soldier emerges from the wood-path, singing.*)

"*Then march to the roll of the drum,*
  It summons the brave to the plain,
Where heroes contend for the home
  Which perchance they may ne'er see again."

(*Pausing abruptly.*) Well, we are finely manned here!

(*1st Soldier re-enters.*)

2nd Sol. How many men do you think we have in all, upon this hill, Edward?

1st Sol. Hist!—more than you count on, perhaps.

2nd Sol. Why? What is the matter? Why do you look among those bushes so earnestly?

1st Student. It is singular, indeed. I can hardly tell you what it is, but twice before in my round, precisely in this same spot, the same impression has flashed upon me, though the sense that gives it, if sense it is, will not bide an instant's questioning. There! Hist! Did nothing move there then?

2nd Sol. I see nothing. This comes of star-gazing, when you should have slept. Though as to that, I have nothing to complain of, certainly. I had to thank your taste that way, last night, for an hour of the most delicious slumber. It was like that we used to snatch of old, between the first stroke of the prayer-bell and its dying peal.

1st Sol. I am glad you could sleep. For myself, such a world of troubled thoughts haunted me, I found more repose in waking.

2nd Sol. Then I wish you could have shared my dream with me, as indeed you seemed to, for you were with me through it all. A blessed dream it was, and yet—

1st Sol. Well, let me share it with you now.

2nd Sol. I cannot tell you how it was, that in honor and good conscience we had effected it, but somehow, methought our part in this sickening warfare was accomplished, and we were home again. Oh the joy of it! oh the joy of it! Even amid my dream, methought we questioned its reality, so unearthly in its perfectness, it seemed. We stood upon the college-green, and the sun was going down with a strange, darkling splendor; and from afar, ever and anon came the thunder roll of battle; but we had nought to do with it; our part was done; our time was out; we were to fight no more. And there we stood, watching the students' games; and there too was poor *Hale*, merry and full of life as e'er he was, for never a thought of his cruel fate crossed my dream. Suddenly we saw two ladies, arm in arm, come swiftly down the shady street, most strangely beautiful and strangely clad, with long white robes, and garlands in their hair, and such a clear and silvery laugh, and something fearful in their loveliness withal; and one of them, as she came smiling toward us—do you remember that bright, fair-haired girl we met in yonder lane one noon? —Just such a smile as hers wore the lady in my dream. Then, into the old chapel we were crowding all; that long-deferred commencement had come on at last; we stood upon a stage, and a strange light filled all the house, and suddenly the ceiling swelled unto the skiey dome, and nations filled the galleries; and I woke, to find myself upon a soldier's couch, and the reveille beating.

1st Sol. Well, if it cheered you, 'twas a good dream most certainly, though, yet—the dream-books might not tell you so. Will you take this glass a moment?

2nd Sol. What is it?

1st Sol. That white house by the orchard, in the door —do you see nothing?

2nd Sol. Yes, a figure, certainly;—yes, now it moves. I had thought those houses were deserted,—it is time they were I think, for all the protection we can give them. How long shall we maintain this post, think you, with such a handful?

1st Sol. Till the preparations below are complete, I trust so at least, for we have watchers in these woods, no doubt, who would speedily report our absence.

2nd Sol. Well, if we all see yonder sun go down, 'tis more than I count on.

1st Sol. A chance if we do—a chance if we do. Will the hour come when this infant nation shall forget her bloody baptism?—the holy name of truth and freedom, that with our hearts' blood we seal upon her in these days of fear?

2nd Sol. Ay, that hour may come.

1st Sol. Then, with tears, and *blood* if need be, shall she learn it anew; and not in vain shall the bones of the martyrs moulder in her peopled vales. For human nature, in her loftiest mood, was this beautiful land of old built, and for ages hid. Here—her cradle-dreams behind her flung; here, on the height of ages past, her solemn eye down their long vistas turned, in a new and nobler life she shall arise here. Ah, who knows but that the book of History may show us at last on its long-marred page—*Man* himself,—no longer the partial and deformed developments of his nature, which each successive age hath left as if in mockery of its ideal,—but, man himself, the creature of thought,—the high, calm, majestic being, that of old stood unshrinking beneath his Maker's gaze. Even, as first he woke amid the gardens of the East, in this far western clime at last he shall smile again,—a perfect thing.

2nd Sol. In your earnestness, you do not mark these strange sounds, Edward. Listen. (*He grasps his sword.*)

(*A Soldier rushes down the path.*)

3d Sol. We are surrounded! Fly. The Indians are upon us. Fly.

[*Rushes on.*

(*Another Soldier bursts from the woods.*)

4th Sol. God! They are butchering them above there, do not stand here!

[*Rushes down the hill.*

2nd Sol. Resistance is vain. Hear those shrieks! There is death in them. Resistance is vain.

1st Sol. Flight is vain. Look yonder! Francis,— the dark hour hath come!

2nd Sol. Is it so? Mother and sister I shall see no more.

(*A number of Indians, disfigured with paint and blood, and brandishing their knives, come rushing down the road, uttering short, fierce yells. Others from below, bringing back the fugitives.*)

1st Sol. We shall die together. God of Truth and Freedom, unto thee our youthful spirits trust we.

(*The Indians surround them. Fighting to the last, they fall.*)

DIALOGUE II.

SCENE. *The deserted house—the chamber—Helen by the table—her head bowed and motionless. She rises slowly from her drooping posture.*

Helen. It is my bridal day. I had forgotten that. (*Looking from the window.*) Is this real? Am I here alone? My mother gone? The army gone? brothers and sisters gone, and those woods full of armed Indians? I am awake. This is not the light of dreams,—'tis the sun that's shining there. Not the fresh arid tender morning sun, that looked in on that parting. Hours he has climbed since then, to turn those shadows thus,—hours that to me were nothing.—Alone?—deserted—defenceless? Of my own will too? There was a *law* in that will, though, was there not? (*Turning suddenly from the window.*) Shall I see him again? The living real of my thousand dreams, in the light of life, will he stand here to-day?—to-day? No, no. Is this swift flow of being leading on to *that*? Oh day of anguish, if in thine awful bosom, still, that dazzling instant sleeps, I can forgive the rest.

(*She stands by the toilette, and begins to gather once more the long hair from her shoulders. Suddenly a low voice at the door breaks the stillness. The Canadian servant looks in.*)

Jan. I ask your pardon—Shall I come in, Ma'amselle?

Helen. Ay, ay, come in. How strangely any voice sounds amid this loneliness. I am glad you are here.

Jan. (*Entering.*) Beautiful! Santa Maria! How beautiful! May I look at these things, Ma'amselle? (*Stopping by the couch strewn with bridal gear.*) Real Brussels! And the plume in this bonnet, was there ever such a lovely droop?

Helen. Come, fasten this clasp for me, Netty. I thought to have had another bridesmaid once, but—that is past— Yes, I am a bride to-day, and I must not wait here unadorned. (*Aside.*) He shall have no hint from me this day of "*altered fortunes.*" As though these weary years had been but last night's dream, and my wedding-day had come as it was fixed, so will I meet him.—Yet I thought to have worn my shroud sooner than this robe.

Jan. This silk would stand alone, Ma'amselle,—and what a lovely white it is! Just such a bodice as this I saw my Lady Mary wear, two years ago this summer, in Quebec; only, this is a thought deeper. But, Santa Maria! how it becomes a shape like yours!

Helen. What a world of buried feeling lives again as I feel the clasp of this robe once more! Will he say these years have changed me?

Jan. (*Aside*) I do not like that altered mien. How the beauty flashes from her? Is it silk and lace that can change one so? Here are bracelets too, Ma'amselle; will you wear them?

Helen. Yes. Go, look from the window, Janette, down the lane to the woods. I am well-high ready now. He will come,—yes, he will come.

(*Janette retreats to the window,—her eye still following the lady.*)

Jan. I have seen brides before, but never so gay a one as this. It is strange and fearful to see her stand here alone, in this lonesome house, all in glistening white, smiling, and the light flashing from her eyes thus. She looks too much like some radiant creature from another world, to be long for this.

Helen. He will come, why should he not? Netty, fix your eye on that opening in the woods, and if you see but a shadow crossing it, tell me quickly.

Jan. I can see nothing—nothing at all. Marie sanctissima!—how quiet it is! The shadows are straight here now, Miss Helen.

Helen. Noon—the very hour has come! Another minute it may be.—Noon, you said, Netty?

(*Joining Janette at the window.*)

Jan. Yes, quite—you can see; and hark, there's the clock. Oh, isn't it lonesome though? See how like the Sunday those houses look, with the doors all closed and the yards and gardens still as midnight. If we could but hear a human voice!—whose, I would not care.

Helen. How like any other noon-day it comes! The faint breeze plays in those graceful boughs as it did yesterday; that little, yellow butterfly glides on its noiseless way above the grass, as then it did;—just so, the shadows sleep on the grassy road-side there;—yes, Netty, yes, *'tis* very lonely.—Hear those merry birds!

Jan. But I would rather hear that signal, Miss Helen, a thousand times, than the best music that ever was played.

Helen. I shall see him again. That wild hope is wild no longer. To doubt were wilder now. Ay, Fate must cross my way with a bold hand, to snatch that good from me now. And yet,—alas, in the shadowy future it lieth still, and a dark and treacherous realm is that! The joys that blossom on its threshold are not ours—It may be, even now, darkness and silence everlasting lie between us.

Jan. Hark—Hark!

Helen. What is it?

Jan. Hark!—There!—Do you hear nothing?

Helen. Distant voices?

Jan. Yes—

Helen. I do—

Jan. Once before,—'twas when I stood in the door below, I heard something like this; but the breeze just then brought the sound of the fall nearer, and drowned it. There it is!—Nearer. The other window, Miss Helen.

Helen. From that hill it comes, does it not?

Jan. Yes—yes, I should think it did. Oh yes. There is a guard left there—I had forgotten that. Mon Dieu! How white your lips are! Are you afraid, Ma'amselle?

(*Helen stands gazing silently from the window.*)

Jan. There is no danger. It must have been those soldiers that we heard,—or the cry of some wild animal roaming through yonder woods—it might have been,—how many strange sounds we hear from them. At another time we should never have thought of it. I think we should have heard that signal though, ere this,—I do, indeed.

Helen. What is it to die? Nor wood nor meadow, nor winding stream, nor the blue sky, do *they* see; nor the voice of bird or insect do they hear; nor breeze, nor sunshine, nor fragrance visits them. Will there be nothing left that makes this being then? The high, Godlike purpose—the life whose breath it is,—can *that* die?—the meek trust in Goodness Infinite,—can *that* perish? No.—This is that building of the soul which nothing can dissolve, that house eternal, that eternity's wide tempests cannot move. No—no—I am not afraid. No—Netty, I am not afraid.

Jan. Will you come here, Miss Helen?

Helen. Well.

Jan. Look among those trees by the road-side—those pine trees, on the side of the hill, where my finger points.—

Helen. Well—what is it?

Jan. Do you see—what a blinding sunshine this is—do you see something moving there?—wait a moment—they are hid among the trees now—you will see them again presently—There!—there they come, a troop of them, see.

Helen. Yes—*Indians*—are they not?

Jan. Ay—it must have been their yelling that we heard.—We need not be alarmed.—They are from the camp—they have come to that spring for water. The wonder is, your soldiers should have let them pass.—You will see them turning back directly now.

Helen. (*Turning from the window.*) Shelter us—all power is thine.

Jan. Holy Virgin!—they are coming this way. Those creatures are coming down that hill, as I live. Yes, there they come.

This strip of wood hides them now. What keeps them there so long? Ay, ay,—I see now—I am sorry I should have alarmed you so, Ma'amselle, for nothing too—They have struck into those woods again, no doubt; they are going back to their camp by the lower route.

Helen. No.

Jan. It must be so. There is no doubt of it. Indeed, we might be sure they would never dare come here.— They cannot know yet that your army are gone. Besides, we should have heard from them ere this. They could never have kept their horrid tongues to themselves so long, I know.—Well, if it were to save me, I cannot screw myself into this shape any longer. (*Rising from the window.*)

Helen. Listen.

Jan. 'Tis nothing but the sound of the river. You can make nothing else of it, Ma'amselle,—unless it is these locusts that you hear. I wish they would cease their everlasting din a moment.

How that breeze has died away! Every leaf is still now! There's not a cloud or a speck in all the sky.

Helen. Look in the west—have you looked there?

Jan. Yes, there are a few little clouds beginning to gather there indeed. We shall have a shower yet ere night.

(*The war-whoop is heard, loud and near.*)

Jan. Mon Dieu! Here they are! It is all over with us! We shall be murdered!

(*She clasps her hands, and shrieks wildly.*)

Helen. Hush! hush! Put down that window, and come away. We must be calm now.

Jan. It is all over with us,—what use is there? Do you hear that trampling?—in the street!—they are coming!

Helen. Janette—Hear me. Will you throw away your life and mine? For shame! Be calm. These Indians cannot know that we are here. They will see these houses *all* deserted. Why should they stop to search *this?* Hush! hush! they are passing now.

Jan. They have stopped!—the trampling has stopped!—I hear the gate,—they have come into the yard.

(*A long wild yell is heard under the window. They stand, looking silently at each other. Again it trembles through the room, louder than before.*)

Helen. I am sorry you stayed here with me. Perhaps—Hark! What was that? What was that? Was it not *Maitland* they said then? It was—it is—Don't grasp me so.

Jan. Nay—what would you do?

Helen. I must speak with them. Let go my arm! Do you not hear? 'Tis Maitland they are talking of. How strangely that blessed name sounds in those tones!

Jan. You must not—we have tempted Heaven already—this is madness.

Helen. Let go, Janette. It is not you they seek. You can conceal yourself. You shall be safe.

Jan. She is wild! Nay, I was mad myself, or I should never have stayed here. It were better to have lived always with them, than to be murdered thus.

(*Helen opens the window, and stands for a moment, looking silently down into the court. She turns away, shuddering.*)

Helen. Can I meet those eyes again?

(*Again the name of Maitland mingles with the wild and unintelligible sounds that rise from without.*)

Helen. Can I? (*She turns to the window.*) What can it mean? His own beautiful steed! How fiercely he prances beneath that unskilful rein. Where's your master, Selma, that he leaves me to be murdered here? A letter! He bids me unfasten the door, Janette.

Jan. And will you?

Helen. They are treacherous I know. This will do.—(*Taking a basket from the toilette.*) Give me that cord. (*She lets down the basket from the window, and draws it up, with a letter in it.*)

Helen. (*Looking at the superscription.*) 'Tis his! I thought so. Is it ink and paper that I want now? (*Breaking it open.*) Ah, there's no forgery in this, 'Tis his! 'tis his!

Jan. How can she stand to look at that little lock of hair now?—smiling as if she had found a bag of diamonds. But there's bad news there. How the color fades out, and the light in her eye dies away. What can it be?

Helen. (*Throwing the letter down, and walking the floor hastily.*) This is too much! I cannot, I cannot, *I cannot go with them*! How could he ask it of me? *This is* cruel.

He knew, perfectly well, how I have always feared them—I cannot go with them.

(She takes up the letter.)

(*Reading.*) "Possible"—"If it were possible"—he does not read that word as I did when I kept this promise—*Possible*? He does not know the meaning that love gives that word—"If I had known an hour sooner," —Ay, ay, an hour sooner!—"Trust me, dear Helen, they will not harm you." *Trust me*, trust me. Won't I?

Jan. She is beckoning them, as I live!

Helen. Bring me that hat and mantle, Netty. I must go with these savages.

Jan. Go with them!

Helen. There is no help for it.

Jan. With these wild creatures,—with these painted devils?—No—Like nothing human they look, I am sure. Ah see, see them in their feathers and blankets, and that long wild hair. See the knives and the tomahawks in their girdles! Holy Mary! Here's one within the court!

Helen. Yes, there he stands—there's life in it now.—There they stand—the chesnut boughs wave over them—this is the filling up of life. They *are* waiting for me. 'Tis no dream.

Jan. Dare you go with them? They will murder you.

Helen. If they were but human, I could move them—and yet it is the human in them that is so dreadful. To die were sad enough—to die by violence, by the power of the innocent elements, were dreadful, or to be torn of beasts; to meet the wild, fierce eye, with its fixed and deadly purpose, more dreadful; but ah, to see the human soul, from the murderers eye glaring on you, to encounter the human will in its wickedness, amid that wild struggle—Oh God! spare me.

Jan. If you fear them so, surely you will not go with them.

Helen. This letter says they are kind and innocent. One I *should* believe tells me there is no cause for fear. In his haste he could not find no other way to send for me.—The army will be here soon,—I *must* go with them.

Jan. But Captain Grey will come back here again this afternoon. Stay,—stay, and we will go with him.

Helen. You can—yes, you will be safe. For myself, I will abide my choice. Surely I need not dread to go where my betrothed husband trusts me so fearlessly. I count my life worth little more than the price at which he values it. Clasp this mantle, Netty.—And is it thus I go forth from these blessed walls at last?—Through all those safe and quiet hours of peace and trust, did this dark end to them lie waiting here?—Are they calling me?

Jan. Yes.

Helen. Well,—I am ready. (*Lingering in the door.*) I shall sit by that window no more. Never again shall I turn those blinds to catch the breeze or the sunshine. Yes—(*returning*), let me look down on that orchard once again. Never more—never more.

(*She walks to the door, again pausing on the threshold.*)

Helen. (*solemnly.*) Oh God, here, from childhood to this hour, morning and evening I have called on thee—forget me not. Farewell, Netty, you will see my mother—you will see them all—that is past.—Tell her I had seen the Indians, and was not afraid.

[*She goes out.*

Jan. It won't take much to make an angel of her, there's that in it.

(*Looking cautiously through the shutters.*)

There she comes! How every eye in that wild group flashes on her! And yet with what a calm and stately bearing she meets them. Holy Mary! she suffers that savage creature to lift her to her horse, as though he were her brother, and the long knife by his side too, glancing in the sunshine! The horse, one would think, he knew the touch of that white hand on his neck. How gently he rears his beautiful head. There they go. Adieu! Was there ever so sad a smile?

Another glimpse I shall have of them yet beyond those trees.—Yes, there they go—there they go. I can see that lovely plume waving among the trees still.—Was there ever so wild a bridal train?

DIALOGUE III.

SCENE. *British Camp. The interior of a Tent richly furnished. An Officer seated at a table covered with papers and maps. A Servant in waiting.*

The Officer. (*Sipping his wine, and carefully examining a plan of the adjacent country.*) About here, we must be—let me see.—I heard the drum from their fort this morning, distinctly. Turn that curtain; we might get a faint breeze there now.

Ser't. But the sun will be coming that side, Sir. It's past two o'clock.

Off. Past two—a good position—very. Well, well,—we'll take our breakfast in Albany on Friday morning, and if our soldiers fast a day or two ere then, why they'll relish it the better;—once in the rich country beyond—Ay, it will take more troops than this General will have at his bidding by that time, to drain the Hudson's borders for us.

(*A Servant enters with a note.*)

Off. (*Reading.*) "*The Baroness Reidesel's compliments—do her the honor—-Voisin has succeeded.*"—Ay, ay,—Voisin has succeeded,—I'll warrant that. That caterer of hers must be in league with the powers of the air, I am certain. General Burgoyne will be but too happy, my Lady—(*writing the answer.*)

[*The Servant goes out.*

Off. Past two! The cannon should be in sight ere this. This to Sir George Ackland.

[*Exit the Attendant.*

Off. Tuesday—Wednesday.—If the batteaux should get here to-morrow. One hundred teams—

(*Another Officer enters the tent.*)

1st Off. How goes it abroad, Colonel St. Leger?

2nd Off. Indeed, Sir, the camp is as quiet as midnight. It's a breathless heat. But there are a few dark heads swelling in the west. We may have a shower yet ere night.

Bur. Good news that. But here is better, (*giving the other an open letter.*)

St. Leger. Ay, ay, that reads well, Sir.

Bur. And here is another as good. Yes Sir, yes Sir,—they are flocking in from all quarters—the insurgents are laying down their arms by hundreds. It must be a miserable fragment that Schuyler has with him by this.

St. L. General Burgoyne, is not it a singular circumstance, that the enemy should allow us to take possession of a point like that without opposition,—so trifling a detachment, too? Why, that hill commands the fort,—certainly it does.

Bur. Well—well. They are pretty much reduced, I fancy, Sir. We shall hardly hear much more from them. Let me see,—this is the hill.

St. L. A pity we could not provoke them into an engagement, though! They depend so entirely upon the popular feeling for supplies and troops, and the whole machinery of their warfare, that it is rather hazardous reckoning upon them, after all. If we could draw them into an engagement *now*, the result would be certain.

Bur. Yes, yes; we must contrive to do that ere long. Rather troublesome travelling companions they make, that's certain. Like those insects that swarm about us here,—no great honor in fighting them, but a good deal of discomfort in letting them alone. We must sweep them out of our way, I think, or at all events give them a brush, that will quiet them a little.

St. L. Or they might prove, after all, like the gadfly in the fable. I do not think this outbreak will be any disadvantage in the end, General.

Bur. Not a whit—not a whit—they have needed this. It will do them good, Sir.

St. L. The fact is, these colonies were founded in the spirit of insubordination, and all the circumstances of their position have hitherto tended to develope only these disorganizing elements.

Bur. It will do them good, Sir. Depend upon it, they'll remember this lesson. Pretty well sickened of war are they all. They'll count the cost ere they try it again.

St. L. We can hardly expect the news from General Reidesel before sunset, I suppose.

Bur. If my messenger returns by to-morrow's sunrise, it is better fortune than I look for.

(*Col. St. Leger goes out.*)

(*Burgoyne resumes his plan.*)

A Ser't. (*At the door.*) Capt. Maitland, Sir.

Bur. Capt. Maitland!

Ser't. From Fort Ann, Sir.

(*Maitland enters.*)

Bur. Captain Maitland! Good heavens, I thought you were at Skeensborough by this,—what has happened? or am I to congratulate myself that the necessity of your embassy is obviated. You met them, perhaps?—

Maitland. There's but little cause of congratulation, Sir, as these dispatches will prove to you. I returned only because my embassy was accomplished.

Bur. Do you mean to say, Captain Maitland, that you have seen the waters of Lake Champlain, since you left here this morning?

Mait. I do, Sir.

Bur. On my word, these roads must have improved since we travelled them some two days agone. I am sorry for your horses, Sir. You saw General Reidesel?

Mait. I left him only at nine o'clock this morning.

(*Burgoyne examines the dispatches.*)

Bur. "Twelve oxen to one batteaux!"—"and but fifty teams!" This news was scarcely worth so much haste, I think,—but fifty teams?—Captain Maitland, had those draught horses from Canada not arrived yet?

Mait. They were just landing this morning as I left, but only one-fourth of the number contracted for.

Bur. Humph! I would like to know what time, at this rate—sit down, Captain Maitland, sit down—we are like to spend the summer here, for aught I see, after all. (*A long pause, in which Burgoyne resumes his reading.*)

Mait. General Burgoyne, I am entrusted with a message from General Reidsel to the Baroness. If this is all—

Bur. What were you saying?—The Baroness—ay, ay—that's all well enough,—but Captain Maitland is aware, no doubt, there are more important subjects on the tapis just now than a lady's behests.

Mait. Sir?—

Bur. (*Pushing the papers impatiently from him.*) This will never do. St. George! We'll give these rebels other work ere many days, than driving away cattle and breaking down bridges for our convenience. Meanwhile we must open some new source of supplies, or we may starve to death among these hills yet. Captain Maitland, I have a proposal to make to you. You are impatient, Sir.

Mait. General Burgoyne!—

Bur. Nay, nay,—there's no haste about it. It were cruel to detain you now, after the toil of this wild journey. You'll find your quarters changed, Captain Maitland. We sent a small detachment across the river just now. Some of our copper-colored allies had got into a fray with the enemy there.

Mait. Ha! (*returning.*)

Bur. Nothing of consequence, as it turns out. We hoped it would have ended in something. A few of the enemy, who were stationed as a guard on a hill not far from Fort Edward, were surprised by a party of Indians, and killed, to a man, I believe. Afterwards, the victors got into a deadly fray among themselves as usual. A quarrel between a couple of these chiefs, at some famous watering place of theirs, and in the midst of it, a party from the fort drove them from the ground;—this is Alaska's own story at least.

Mait. Alaska's!

Bur. Alaska?—Alaska?—yes, I think it was,—one of these new allies we have picked up here.

Mait. (*In a whisper.*) Good God!

Bur. By the time our detachment arrived there, however, the ground was cleared, and they took quiet possession. Are you ill, Captain Maitland?

Mait. A little,—it is nothing. I am to cross the river.

Bur, Yes. You will take these papers to Captain Andre. You have over-fatigued yourself. You should have taken more time for this wild journey.

(*Maitland goes out.*)

Bur. I do not like the idea of division, but it cannot be helped now. This gallant young soldier were a fitting leader for such an enterprize.

DIALOGUE IV.

SCENE. *The ground before Maitland's Tent.*

(*Maitland and the Indian Chief, Manida, enter.*)

Mait. This is well. (*He writes on a slip of paper, and gives it to the Indian.*) Take that, they will give you the reward you ask for it. Let me see your face no more, that is all.

Manida. Ha, *Monsieur*?

Mait. Let me see your face no more, I say. Do you understand me?

Manida. (*Smiling.*) Oui.

(*Maitland turns from him. The Indian goes off in the opposite direction. He stops a moment, and steals a look at Maitland,—throws his head back with a long silent laugh, and then goes on toward the woods.*)

Mait. (*Musing.*) I like this. *This* is womanly! Nay, perhaps there is no caprice about it. I may have misinterpreted that letter in my haste last night. Very likely. Well,—better this, than that Helen Grey should come to evil through fault of mine,—better this, than the anguish of the horrible misgivings that haunted me amid my journey.

And so pass these faery visions! Nay, not thus. It will take longer than this to unlink this one day's hope from its thousand fastnesses. I thought, ere this, to have met the spirit of those beaming eyes, to have taken to my heart for ever this soft, pure being of another life. And yet, even as I rode through those lonely hills this morning, with every picture my hope painted, there came a strange misgiving;—like some scene of laughing noonday loveliness, darkening in the shadow of a summer's cloud.

Strange that Alaska should abandon my trust! I cannot understand it. Why, I should never have trusted her with this rascal Indian. There was something in his eye, hateful beyond all thought,—and once or twice I caught a strange expression in it, like malignant triumph it seemed. It may be—no, he must have seen her—that glove he showed me was hers, I know. Good God!—what if—I think my old experience should have taught me there was little danger of her risking much in my behalf. Well—even this is better, than that Helen Grey should have come to evil through fault of mine.

PART SIXTH

RECONCILIATION.

DIALOGUE I.

SCENE. *The slope of the Hill near Fort Edward. The road-side, shaded with stately pines and hemlocks.*

(*Two British Officers, coming slowly down the road.*)

1st Off. Yes, here has been wild work upon this hill to-day. They were slaughtered to a man.

2nd Off. I saw a sight above there, just now, that sickened me of warfare.

1st Off. And what was that, pry'thee?

2nd Off. Oh nothing,—'twas nothing but a dead soldier; a common sight enough, indeed; but this was a mere youth;—he was lying in a little hollow on the roadside, and as I crossed in haste, I had well-nigh set my foot on his brow. Such a brow it was, so young, so noble, and the dark chesnut curls clustering about it. I think I never saw a more classic set of features, or a look of loftier courage than that which death seemed to have found and marbled in them. Hark—that's a water-fall we hear.

1st Off. I saw him, there was another though, lying not far thence, the sight of whom moved me more. He was younger yet, or seemed so, and of a softer mould; and, torn and bloody as they were, I fancied I could see in his garb and appointments, and in every line of his features, the traces of some mother's tenderness.

2nd Off. Listen, Andre! This is beautiful! There's some cascade not far hence, worth searching for.

Andre. Yes, just in among those trees you'll find a perfect drawing-room, carpeted, canopied, and dark as twilight; its verdant seats broidered with violets and forget-me-nots; and all untenanted it seems, nay, deserted rather, for the music wastes on the lonely air, as if the fairy that kept state there, in gossip mood had stolen down some neighboring aisle, and would be home anon. I would have bartered all the glory of this campaign for leave to stretch myself on its mossy bank, for a soft hour or so.

Mor. Ay, with Chaucer or the "Faery Queen." If one could people these lovely shades with the fresh creations of the olden time, knight and lady, and dark enchantress and Paynim fierce, instead of Yankee rebels—

Andre. 'Twere well your faery-work were of no lasting mould, or these same Yankee rebels would scarce thank you for your pains,—they hold that race in little reverence. Alas,—

    No grot divine, or wood-nymph haunted glen,
    Or stream, or fount, shall these young shades e'er know.
    No beautiful divinity, stealing afar
    Through darkling nooks, to poet's eye thence gleam;
    With mocking mystery the dim ways wind,
    They reach not to the blessed fairy-land
    That once all lovely in heaven's stolen light,
    To yearning thoughts, in the deep green-wood grew.
    Ah! had they come to light when nature
    Was a wonder-loving, story-telling child!—
    The misty morn of ages had gone by,
    The dreamy childhood of the race was past,
    And in its tame and reasoning manhood,
    In the daylight broad, and noon-day of all time,
    This world hath sprung. The poetry of *truth*,
    None other, shall her shining lakes, and woods,
    And ocean-streams, and hoary mountains wear.
    Perchance that other day of poesy,
    Unsung of prophets, that upon the lands
    Shall dawn yet, thence shall spring. The self-same mind
    That on the night of ages once, for us
    Those deathless clusters flung, the self-same mind,
    With all its ancient elements of might,
    Among us now its ancient glory hides;
    But, from its smothered power, and buried wealth,
    A golden future sparkles, decked from deeper founts,
    A new and lovelier firmament,
    A thousand realms of song undreamed of now,
    That shall make Romance a forgotten world,
    And the young heaven of Antiquity,
    With all its starry groups, a gathered scroll.

Mor. Ay, Andre, you were born a poet, and have mistaken your art. Prythee excuse me, who am but a poor soldier, for marring so fine a rhapsody with any thing so sublunary; but, methinks, for an enemy's quarters, yonder fort shows as peaceable a front of stone and mortar as one could ask for. What can it mean that they are so quiet there?

Andre. That spy did not return a second time.

Mor. The rogues have made sure of him ere this, I fancy. They may have given us the slip,—who knows?

Andre. I would like to venture a stroll through that shady street if I thought so. A dim impression that I have somewhere seen this view before, haunts me unaccountably.

Mor. How I hate that sober, afternoon air, that hangs like an invisible presence over it all. You can see it in the sunshine on those white walls, you can hear it in the hum of the bee from the bending thistle here.

Andre. Of the mind it is. This were lovely as the morning light, but for the shade it gathers thence, from the thought of decline and the vanishing day. 'Tis a pretty spot.

Mor. Yes, but the quiet goings-on of life are all hushed there now.

Andre. Ay, this is the hour, when the home-bound children swing the gate with a merry spring, and the mother sits at her work by the open window, with her quiet eye, and the daughter, with the beauty of an untamed soul in her's, looks forth on the woods and meadows, and thinks of her walk at even-tide. I thought it was something like a memory that haunted me thus,—'tis the spot that Maitland talked of yesterday.

Mor. Captain Maitland? I saw him just now at the works above.

Andre. Here? On this hill?

Mor. Yes,—something struck me in his mien,—and there he stands with Colonel Hill, above, on the other side.—Mark him now. Your friend is handsome, Andre; he is handsome, I'll own,—but I never liked that smile of his, and I think I like it less than ever now.

Andre. Why, that's the genuine Apollo-curl,—a line's breadth deeper were too much, I'll own.

(*Maitland and another Officer enter.*)

Off. That is all,—that is all, I believe, Captain Maitland. Yonder pretty dwelling among the trees seems an old acquaintance of yours. It has had the ill manners to rob me of your eye ever since we stood here, and I have had little token that the other senses were not in its company. Andre, has your friend never a ladye-love in these wilds, you could tell us of?

Mor. He is sworn to secresy. Did you mark that glance?

Mait. Love! I hold it a pretty theme for the ballad-makers, Colonel Hill; but for myself, I have scarce time for rhyming just now. Captain Andre, here are papers for you.

[*He walks away, descending the road.*

Col. Hill. So! So! What ails the boy?

(*Looking after him for a moment, and then ascending the hill.*)

Andre. (*Reading.*) Humph! Here's prose enough! Will you walk up the hill with me, Mortimer? I must cross the river again.

Mait. First let me seek this horse of mine,—the rogue must have strayed down this path, I think.

(*He enters the wood.*)

(*Andre walks to and fro with an impatient air, then pauses.*)

Andre. Well, I can wait no longer for this loiterer.

[*Exit.*

(*Mortimer re-enters, calling from the woods.*)

Mor. Andre! Maitland! Colonel Hill! Good Heavens! Where the devil are they all? Maitland!

(*Maitland appears, slowly ascending the road.*)

Mor. For the love of Heaven,—come here.

Mail. Nay.—but what is it?

Mor. For God's sake, come,

DIALOGUE II.

SCENE. *A little glen, darkly shaded with pines. A fountain issuing from one side, and falling with a curious murmur into the basin below.*

(*Mortimer and Maitland enter.*)

Mor. This is the place!—Well, if hallucinations like this can visit mortal eyes, I'll ne'er trust mine again. 'Tis the spot, I'm sure of it,—the place, too, that Andre was raving about just now.—The fairies' drawing-room,—palace rather,—look at these graceful shafts, Maitland,—and fairies' work, it must have been in good earnest.

Mait. If it's to admire this clump of pine trees you have brought me hither, allow me to say you might have spared yourself that trouble. I have seen the place already, as often as I care to.

Mor. Come this way a little,—yes, it was just above there that I stood,—it must have been.

Mait. If you would give me some little inkling of what you are talking about, Lieutenant Mortimer, I should be more likely to help you, if it's help you need.

Mor. I do not ask you to believe me, but,—as I was springing on my horse just now above there, the gurgling of this spring caught my ear, and looking down suddenly—upon my word, Captain Maitland, I am ashamed to describe what cannot but seem to you such an improbable piece of fancy-work; and yet, true it seemed, as that I see you now. I was looking down, as I said, when suddenly, among those low evergreens, the brilliant hue of a silken mantle caught my eye, and then a woman's brow gleamed up upon me. Yes, there in that dark cradle, calmly sleeping, all flashing with gold and jewels, like some bright vision of olden time, methought there lay—a lady,—a girl, young and lovely as a dream;—the white plume in her bonnet soiled and broken, and the long bright hair streaming heavily on her mantle,—and yet with all its loveliness, such a face of utter sorrow saw I never. I *saw* her, I saw her, as I see you now,—the proud young form with such a depth of grace, in its strange repose, and—where are you going?—what are you doing, Maitland?

Mait. Helen Grey!—

Mor. You are right. I did not mark that break—yes—there she lies. Said I right, Maitland?

Mait. Helen Grey!—

Mor. Maitland! Heavens!—what a world of anguish that tone reveals!—Why do you stand gazing on that lovely sleeper thus?

Mait. Bring water. There's a cup at yonder spring. Here has been treachery! Devils and fiends have been working here against me. We must unclasp this mantle. The treasure of the earth lies here.—Now doth mine arm enfold it once, at last. 'Tis sweet, Helen, mine own *true* love; 'tis sweet, even thus.

Mor. This letter,—see—from those loosened folds it just now dropped. This might throw some light, perchance—

Mait. Let it be. There's light enough. I want no more. Water,—more water,—do you see?

Mor. Maitland,—this is vain. Mark this dark spot upon her girdle—

Mait. Hush, hush,—there, cover it thus—'tis nothing, Loosen this bonnet—so—'twas a firm hand that tied that knot; so—she can breathe now.

Mor. How like life, those soft curls burst from their loosened pressure! But mark you—there is no other motion, I am sorry to distress you,—but—Maitland—this lady is dead.

Mait. Dead! Lying hell-hound! *Dead*! Say that again.

Mor. God help you!

Mait. Dead! Helen Grey, open these eyes. Here's one that, never having seen them, talks of death. Oh God! is it thus we meet at last? At last these arms are round her, and she knows it not. I look upon her, but her eye answers me not. Dead!—for me? Murdered!—mine own hand hath done it.

Mor. Why do you start thus?

Mait. Hush!—hush! There!—again—that slow heavy throb—again! again!

Mor. Good God! she breathes! This is life indeed.

Mait. (*Solemnly*.) Ay, thank God. This moment's sweetness is enough.

Mor. How like one in troubled sleep she murmurs! Mark those tones of sweet and wild entreaty. Listen!

Mait. I have heard it again!—from the buried years of love and hope that music came. She is here. 'Tis *she*. This is no marble mockery. She is here! Her head is on my bosom. Death cannot rob me of this sweetness now.

(*Talking without*.)

A Lady. This way—I hear their voices. Down this pathway—here they are.

(*Lady Ackland and Andre enter the Glen*.)

Lady A. I knew it could not be. They told us she was murdered, Maitland. (*Starting back*.) Ah—ah—God help thee, Maitland!

Mait. Listen, listen. She was speaking but now. There—again!

Lady A. And this is she! Can the wilderness blossom thus? And did God unfold such loveliness—for a waste so cruel?

Helen. (*In a low murmur*.) We are almost there. If we could but pass this glen. Oh God! will they stop here? Go on,—go on. Was not that a white tent I saw? Go on. They will not. 'Tis nothing,—do not weep.

Mait. Look at me, Helen.—Open these eyes. One more look—one more.

Andre. She hears your bidding.

Mait. Oh God! Do you see those eyes—those dim, bewildered eyes?—it is quenched—quenched. Let her lean on you.

Lady A. Gently—gently, she does not see us yet.

Helen. Oh Mother, I am ill and weary. Here's this dream again! Blue sky? and pine-tree boughs? Am I here indeed? Yes, I remember now,—we stood upon that cliff—I am dying. Is there no one here? Whose tears are these?

Lady A. Dear child, sweet one, nay, lean on me.

Helen. My mother, oh my mother, come to me. Come, Annie, come, come! Strangers all!

Mor. Her eye is on him. Hush!

Andre. See in an instant how the light comes flashing up from those dim depths again. *That* is the eye that I saw yesterday.

Lady A. That slowly settling smile,—deeper and deeper—saw you ever any thing so gay, so passing lovely?

Helen. Is it—is it—Everard Maitland—is it *thee*? The living real of my thousand dreams, in the light of life doth he stand there now? Doth he? *'Tis he!*

Mait. Helen!

Helen. 'Tis he! That tone's spell builds around me its all-sheltering music-walls, and death is nothing. Oh God, when at thy dark will dimly revealed, I trembled yesterday, I did not think in this most rosy bower to meet its fearfulness.

Mait. Helen,—dost thou love me *yet*?

Helen. Doubter, am I dying here?

Mait. 'Tis her own most rich and blessed smile, even as of old in mirth it shone upon me. Your murderer, you count me then?

Helen. Come hither,—let me lean on *you*. Star of the wilderness!—of this life that is fading now, the sun!—*doth* mine eye see thee, then, at last? Oh! this is sweet! On its own holy home my head rests now. Everard, in this dark world *Love leans on Faith*. How else, even in God's love and loveliness, could I trust now for that strange future on whose bloody threshold I am lying here; yes, and in spite of prayers and trust, and struggling hopes. And yet—how beautiful it is—that love invisible, invisible no more. Like glorious sunshine it is streaming round me,—lighting all. The infinite of that thy smile hath imaged, as real,—it beams on me now. Have faith, in *him* I mean; for—if we meet again—we'll need it then no more; and—how dim it grows—nay, let me lean on you,—and—through *this* life's darkening glass I shall see you no more. Nay, hold me!—quick!—where art thou?—Everard!—He is gone—gone!

Lady A. Dead!—

Mor. She is dead!

Andre. This was Love.

Lady A. See how her eyes are fixed on *you*. The light and love of the vanished soul looks through them still. Cruelly hath it been sent thence; and no other gleam of its changeful beauty will e'er dawn in them. Sadly, oh lovely stranger, I close for ever now these dark-fringed lids upon their love and beauty. Yes—*this* was love!

Andre. And so there was a need-be in its doom. I'll ne'er believe *that* genuine, that is blessed. The fate of this life would not suffer it. Ah! if it would, if Heaven should leave a gem like that outside her walls, we should none of us go thither.

Mait. Dead? How beautiful! Yes—let her lie there—under that lovely canopy. Dead!—it's a curious word—How comes it that we all stand here? Ha, Andre?—is it you?

Andre. I heard the tale as I crossed just now, from an Indian, who was one in the ambuscade this noon—and in the woods on the other side, I found this lady, with her attendants, abiding the promise she made you last night, to welcome this lovely stranger with her savage guides.

Mait. Hush, hush. Let it pass. See,—a bride!

Mor. (*Aside.*) Did he trust her with these murderers?

Mait. Ay—say yes.

Andre. Indeed, Maitland, you wrong yourself. It was the treachery of this savage Manida that crossed your plans, working the mission of some Higher power,—as for Alaska, you might as soon have doubted me.

The Chief he sent for her was one he had known years—but, unfortunately, he was one in the ambuscade this morning—nay, the leader of it; for the murdered Indian was his son; and meanwhile amid the fight the treacherous Manida, who accompanied him to Maitland's tent last night, and heard the promised reward, found means to steal from its concealment the letter, with which he easily won this trusting lady to accompany him.

Mor. Ah!—there it lies.

Andre. It was here in this glen that Alaska, discovering the treachery, lay in wait for them with a band of chosen warriors, and on that cliff above they fought.

Lady A. (*Aside.*) And she stood there, amid those yelling demons alone! Methinks the angels should have come from their unseen dwellings at her prayer. Can our humanity's darkest extremity wring no love from the invisible?—

Andre. Alaska had regained his charge; but the malignant eye, and the deadly arrow of the vanquished Indian followed her. She fell, even in the place where you found her; for at that same instant a party from the fort drove them hence, victor and vanquished. Alaska fled; but the murderer, with a tale cunning enough to deceive the lover, boldly demanded and obtained the prize.

Mor. Mark his changed mien. I would rather see tears for a grief like this, than that calm smile with which he gazes on her now.

(*Burgoyne and St. Leger are seen talking in the road above,—they enter the glen.*)

Bur. At a crisis like this we might better have lost a thousand men in battle! Ah! ah!—a sight for our enemies, Lady Ackland! Where is this Indian?

St. L. We have sent out for him. No one has seen him as yet.

Bur. Let him be found. Look to it. We will give them an example for once. I say, at a crisis like this we might better have lost a thousand men in battle, for it will turn thousands against us, and rouse the slumbering spirit of resistance here, at the very crisis when, had it slumbered on a little longer, all was ours.

St. L. But this was a quarrel among the Indians, and no fault of ours.

Bur. No matter. You will see what Schuyler will make of it. His wordy proclamation will have its living sequel now. A young and innocent girl, seeking the protection of our camp, is inhumanly murdered by Indians in our pay. A single tale like this is enough to undo at a blow all that we have accomplished here. With ten thousand wild aggravations, it will be told in every cottage of these borders before to-morrow's sunset.

(*Another Officer enters hastily.*)

Off. Here is Arnold, with a thousand men, on the brow of the next hill. One of the rebel guard escaped, and the news of the massacre here has reached their camp below.

Bur. Said I right?

(*The three Officers go out together.*)

Andre. This story is spreading fast, there will be throngs here presently. Maitland,—nay, do not let me startle you thus, but—

Mait. Is it you? What was it we were saying yesterday?—we should have noted it. This were a picture worth your pencilling now. Those silken vestments,—that long, golden hair,—this youthful shape,—there's that same haughty grace about it, that the smile of these thought-lit eyes would disown with every glance. Then that letter,—and the Lady Ackland here,—Weeping?—This is most strange. I know you all,—but,—as I live I can't remember how this chanced. How comes it that we all stand here? Pearls?—and white silk?—a bridal?—Ha ha ha! (*Laughing wildly.*)

Lady A. Take me away. This is too terrible! lean stay here no longer. Take me away, Andre.

[*Exeunt Andre and Lady A.*

(*An Officer enters.*)

The Officer. We are ordered to withdraw our detachment, Captain Maitland. The rebels are just below, some two thousand strong, and in no mood to be encountered.

Mor. He does not hear you. We must leave that murdered lady here, and 'tis vain to think of parting them. Come.

[*Exeunt Mortimer and Officer.*

Mait. They are gone at last. They are all gone. I am alone with my dead bride. I must needs smile—I could not weep when those haughty and prying eyes were upon me, but now—I am alone with my dead bride.—Helen, they are all gone,—we are alone. How still she lies,—smiling too,—on that same bank. She will speak, surely she will. How lightly those soft lashes lie, as if a word would lift them.—Helen!—I will be calm and patient as a child. This lovely smile is deepening, it will melt to words again.—Hark! that spring,—that same curious murmur! We have checked our sweetest words to hear it, we have stood here listening to it, till we fancied, in its talk-like tones, wild histories, beautiful and sad, the secrets of the woods.—Oh God!—and have such memories no power here now? In mine ear alone doth the spring murmur now. Death! what is't?—Awake! awake,—by the love that is *stronger* than death,—awake!—

I thought that scene would shift. It had a heavy, dream-like mistiness. *This* is reality again. *These* are the pine trees that I dreamed of. See! how beautiful! With the sharp outline and the vivid hue such as our childhood's unworn sense yields, they are waving now. Look, Andre, there she sits, the young and radiant stranger,—there, in the golden sunset she is sitting still, braiding those flowers,—see, how the rich life flashes in her eye, and yet, just now I dreamed that she was dead, and—and—Oh my God!

(*A voice without.*)

Let go, who stays me?—where's my sister?

(*Captain Grey enters.*)

Grey. Ha! Murderer! art satisfied?

Mait. Ay.

Grey. What, do you mock me, Sir?

Mait. Let her be. She is mine!—all mine! my love, my bride,—my *bride*?—*Murderer*?—Stay!—Don't glare at me! I know you, Sir. I can hurl off these mountain shadows yet.—They'll send some stronger devil ere they wrench this hold from me! I know you well. What make you here?

Grey. Madness!—there's little wonder!—It's the only good that Heaven has left for him! My lovely playfellow,—my sister, is it so indeed? Alas! all gently lies this hand in mine. There is no angry strength here now. Helen!—Ah! would to God our last words had not been in bitterness.

Mait. He weeps. I never thought to see tears there. List!—she should not lie there thus. Strange it should move you so!—Think it a picture now. 'Tis but a well-wrought painting after all, if one but thinks so. See,—'tis but a sleeping girl, with the red summer light upon her cheek, and the slight breeze stirring her golden hair. Mark you that shoulder's grace?—They come.

(*Leslie, Elliston, and others enter.*)

Leslie. Oh God, was there none other? My lovely cousin, and—were *you* the victim? In your bridal glory chosen,—nay, with your heart's holiest law lured to the bloody altar! Yet this day's history, and something in that calm, high mien, tells me, as freely you had moved unto it, though God had spoken by a higher voice, and with a martyr's garland beckoned you.

Elliston. Our cause is linked unto that ancient one, the cause of Love and Truth; in which Heaven moves with unrelenting hand, not sparing its own loveliest ones, but unto bloody death freely delivering them.

(*Grey and Leslie converse apart.*)

Leslie. Yes—we will bury her here. 'Tis a fitting spot; and unto distant days, this lonely grave, with its ever-verdant canopy, shall be even as Love's Shrine. Thither, in the calm and smiling summers of those bloodless times shall many a fair young pilgrim come, to wonder at such love; and living eyes shall weep, and living hearts shall heave over its cruel fate, when unto her the long-told tale, and all the anguish of this far-off day, shall be even as the dim passage of some troubled dream. A martyr's garland she hath won indeed; true Love's young Martyr there she lies.

Elliston. Yet was that love but the wreathed and glittering weapon of a higher doom. In that holy cause, whose martyrs strew a thousand fields, truth's, freedom's, God's, darkly, by *Power Invisible* hath this young life been offered here.

A thousand graves like this, over all this lovely land, in lanes and fields, on the lonely hill-side, by the laughing stream, and in the depths of many a silent wood, to distant days shall speak—of blood-sealed destinies; with voices that no tyrant's power can smother, they shall speak.—

Leslie. The light of that chamber window, through the soft summer evening will shine here; no mournful memory of all the lovely past will it waken. The autumn blaze will flicker within those distant walls, and gather its pleasant circle again; but *she* will lie calmly here. For ever at her feet the river of her childhood shall murmur on, and many a lovely spring-time, like the spring-times of her childhood, shall come and go, but no yearning hope shall it waken here; the winter shall sing through the desolate boughs, and rear its fairy temples around her, but nought shall break her dreamless rest.—

Mait. Graves! Is it graves they are talking of? Will they bury this gay young bride! 'Tis but the name; there's nothing sad in it. In the lovely summer twilight shall her burial be, and thus; in all her bridal array, with the glory of the crimson sunset shining through the trees;—see what a fearful glow is kindling on her cheek, and that faint breeze—or, is it life that stirs these curls? Stay!—whose young brow is this?—Ha!—*whose* smile is this? Who is this they would hurry away into the darkness of death? The grave! Could you fold the rosy and all-speading beauty of heaven in the narrow grave? Helen, is it thee?—my heaven, my long-lost heaven; and, even now, but for mine own deed—Oh God! was there no hand but mine?—but for me—They —shall not utter it,—there, thus. There's but *one* cry that could unfold this grief, but that would circle the round universe and fill eternity. A sad sight this! Is't known who killed this lady, Sir?

Leslie. Of all the wrecks of beautiful humanity that strew these paths, we have found none so sad as this!

Elliston. Mark you those groups of soldiers loitering on the road-side there?

An Officer. Curiosity. The regiment that was dismissed to-day. They'll be here anon.

Leslie. Ay, let them come.

Off. Look,—who comes up that winding pathway through the trees, with such a swift and stately movement? A woman! See how the rude soldiers turn aside with awe. Ah, she comes hither.

(*A voice without.*)

Where is she?—stand aside!—What have you here in this dark ring?—Henry—nay, let me come.

(*Mrs. Grey enters the glen.*)

Grey. For God's sake, Madam, let me lead you hence. This is no place for you. Look at this group of men, officers, soldiers—

Mrs. G. Would you cheat me *thus*? Is it no place for *me*? What kind of place is't then for her, whose— Oh God!—think you I do not see that slippered foot, nor know whose it is,—and whose plumed bonnet is it that lies crushed there at their feet?—unhand me, Henry.

Leslie. Nay, let her come,—'tis best.

(*She passes swiftly through the parting group.*)

Mrs. G. My daughter!—Blood? My stricken child smile you? No pity was there then? Speak to me, speak! Your mother's tears are on your brow, and heed you not? Nay, tell me all, my smitten one. This day's dark history will you never pour into my ear, that hath treasured so often your lightest grief? Alone through that wild anguish have you passed, and smile you now? I bade her trust in God. Did *God* see this?

(*Arnold, and a group of Soldiers, enter the glen.*)

Arnold. Look there. Ay, ay, look there. You were right, Leslie;—this *is* better than a battle-field. They'll find that this day's work will cost them dear.

Mrs. G. Did *God*, who loves as mothers love their babes, see this I Had I been there, with my love, in the heavens, could *I* have given up this innocent and tender child a prey to the wild Indians? No!—and legions of pitying angels waiting but my word. No,—no.

Elliston. Had you been there,—from that far centre whence God's eye sees all, you had beheld what lies in darkness here. Forth from this fearful hour you might have seen Peace, like a river, flowing o'er the years to come; and smiles, ten thousand, thousand smiles, down the long ages brightening, sown in this day's tears. Had you been there with God's *all*-pitying eye, the pitying legions had waited your word in vain, for once, unto a sterner doom, for the world's sake he gave his Son.

Mrs. G. Words! Look there. That mother warned me yesterday. "*Words, words! My own child's blood,*"—I *see* it now.

(*A group of Soldiers enter.*)

A. Soldier. (*Whispering.*) Who would have thought to see tears on *his* face; look you, Jack Richards.

Another Sol. 'Twas his sister, hush!—

Arnold. Ay, ay, come hither. Look you there! Lay down your arms. Seek the royal mercy;—here it is. Your wives, your sisters, and your innocent children;—let them seek the royal shelter;—it is a safe one. See.

3d Sol. It was just so in Jersey last winter;—made no difference which side you were.

Arnold. Ask no reasons.—'Twas in sport may be. 'Tis but one, in many such. Shameless tyranny we have borne long, and now, for resistance, to red butchery we are given over. The sport of lawless soldiers, and savages more cruel than the fiends in hell, are we, and the gentle beings of our homes;—but, 'tis the Royal power. Lay down your arms.

Soldiers. (*Shouting.*) *No.*

Arnold. Nay, nay,—in its caprice some will be safe,—it may not light on you. See, here's the proclamation. (*Throwing it among them.*) Pardon for rebles.

Soldiers. No—no. (*Shouting.*) Away with pardon!—(*Tearing the proclamation.*) To the death! Freedom for ever!